Pr

D

1ˢᵗ Prize

"This is an atmospheric and ...

Afghanistan. While a host of personalities flit in and out of the story, the enduring character is Afghanistan itself... as if the land is a slumbering giant that the protagonists are afraid to awake. It is the enduring enigma of the work that sets it apart - the deft handling of metaphor and rhythm, an understanding of language and a creative facility that raises it far above the other entries."

Jake Wallis Simons

Working Away

Adult Prose and Overall Winner Neil Gunn

"We were all struck by the combination of grace, technique, empathy, feeling and control that made this intensely moving story work... I can feel it still."

(Lead Judge) **Andrew Greig**

Aftermath

1ˢᵗ Prize Woman and Home Short Story

"Moving and perceptive, with clever use of minute detail to convey atmosphere and emotion."

Barbara Couvela

Sow the Wind

Finalist Booktown Writers Short Story

"A beautifully drawn moment in time of a couple in crisis - with real emotional heft."

Michael Malone

Also by Margaret Skea

Scottish Historical Fiction:

Turn of the Tide: Munro Saga 1 - Beryl Bainbridge Best First Time Novelist Award 2014

A House Divided: Munro Saga 2 - Long-list Historical Novel Society New Novel Award 2016

By Sword and Storm: Munro Saga 3 (DOP July 2018)

Katharina series:

Katharina: Deliverance

Katharina: Fortitude (DOP early 2019)

Margaret Skea was born in Ulster and now lives with her husband in the Scottish Borders. An Hawthornden fellow, accomplished speaker, Creative Writing tutor and workshop leader, she is currently working on her fifth novel. Many of her short stories have won or been placed in competitions and published in magazines and anthologies at home and abroad, but others have remained in a drawer of her desk. She has been repeatedly asked if she would bring out an anthology. This collection is the result.

Dust Blowing

An Anthology of Short Stories

Margaret Skea

sanderling

First published by Sanderling Books in 2016

A CIP catalogue record of this book is available from the British Library.

Paperback ISBN: 978-0-9933331-2-5
E-book ISBN: 978-0-9933331-3-2
Printed in Great Britain

Sanderling Books
28 Riverside Drive
Kelso
Roxburghshire
Scotland
TD5 7R

Table of Contents

Dust Blowing..7
Winner: Winchester; Shortlist: Fish

Letters (from America, Mostly) 15

Battenberg for Tea..36

Magda's War..49
Longlist: Historical Novel Society

Gulls Calling 67

On Pharmacy Road 77
3rd: Rubery; Shortlist: Mslexia

Celebrity Status...89
Longlist: Matthew Pritchard

Aftermath..99
1st Prize Woman and Home

Finding Rose 109

We Need to Talk..123

Sow the Wind 133
Shortlist: Booktown Writers

Working Away...144
Adult Prose and Overall Winner Neil Gunn

Dust Blowing

Dawn is a long time coming. It will be colder today. Ahmed is hunched over the fire and I am hunched at the mouth of my tent. Last night I could not sleep and Ahmed would not. He stayed close, but not too close, wrapped tight in his patched burnous, his body blocking the worst of the growing North wind.

In the last nine hours - is it only nine hours? - each time I looked up he turned to me, his dark eyes barely focused, seeming as if he were about to speak, but did not. Last night, he said kindly, "David, there is but a single donkey now, and every day the snow is nearer."

That is all.

I know, I know. The border is at least three days away, the distant guns and bombs never stop, and yes, I know that the first winter snow is a week overdue, that we cannot force our way through if it comes. But Ahmed, dear, stupid, old man, do you really think that makes me feel *better?*

Around us the camp is stirring, silence separating into small sounds: the rhythmic flapping of canvas, sandals scuffling the hard-packed earth, a baby grizzling, unable to feed. I move towards the fire, where Ahmed coaxes a flame from cigarette-sized curls of smoke, shielding it from the gusting of the wind until it burns steadily, the odour of donkey dung hanging pungent in the air.

Ahmed glances upward as my shadow falls across him, his eyes betraying nothing. He nods and gestures towards the half-empty water-bag. I crouch beside him and tip my head to trickle water into my mouth, swilling it round and round, trying to swell the volume with saliva, to wash the grit from between my teeth, the fur from my tongue. I dare not take much, for last night we collected only what little we could distil from the dew that fell with dusk.

We did not have the heart to dig.

A handful of children drift towards the fire and huddle close, rubbing with raw knuckles at the smoke spiralling into their eyes. They no longer play in the hour before we break camp. When we began this journey I would wake to scuffles and giggles outside my tent, with Nazim, always more forward than the rest, poking a stick through a finger-picked gap in the rough lacing to prod the soles of my feet stretched out beyond the thin blankets. I used to lie, pretending sleep, for just long enough, then rise with a roar, scattering the children beyond arm's length, their laughter high and infectious.

There is no laughter now. No Nazim.

Between the tents, in the bare space that counts for community here, the women, surrounded by opened bundles, sort the remains of their lives into two unequal piles. The discard pile grows, while what we can carry with us shrivels to less than necessity. With only one donkey remaining, there is nothing else to do.

Last autumn, swelled with responsibility, I led donkeys roped together in strings of twenty or more - heaped with blankets, medicines and foods - aid transferred from the UNICEF lorries halted at Chitral. We crossed by the Shah Saleem pass, driving high into the mountains, playing at 'cat and mouse' with winter and the warlords.

And though both chase us still, this is a very different journey.

Then we travelled northwards, clawing our way along paths no wider than our shoulders, scree slithering beneath our feet, stones scattering into the valley below. Often the leading donkey, shying at hidden bogies, would stop and refuse to budge, so that the others bunched up behind him, nipping haunches, stamping and kicking, their cargo swaying dangerously. Ahmed would scrabble past from the rear, like a mountain goat, alternately cajoling and cursing, pushing while I pulled, beating the donkey while I tempted it with sugar, until, without warning, it would flick its ears and lurch forward, butting me in the stomach, so that I fell sprawling in the dust, while it stepped over me delicately and plodded on.

Ahmed's laughter irritated me then. I would welcome it now.

As I get up the women raise their eyes, but there is no life in them. They do not say so, but I have helped to make it thus. One mother rolling a pillow deftly, one-handed, is with the other gently stroking the cheek of her child, who curls foetus-like, on a blanket by her side, coughing fitfully, his chest jerking. I look away for fear that I will see stirring a new appeal. It would be easier for me if they still wore the burqa, but perhaps I do not deserve ease. Something of them all died with Nazim. Something in me also.

Their eyes drop again to their children, but they do not ask for food, for they know there is none to give.

Behind me, Ahmed has begun to strike the tents. When I join him we work together silently, releasing the ropes and pulling free the poles, so that the canvases slump to the ground, reminding me of the camels in the souk at Chaghcharah, when caravans still passed through the Ghowr. It is not so very long ago, but the world has changed, as I have. We pack the tents tightly, in stout bundles. I envy Ahmed, who will carry his with ease, belying his greater age, walking with the long, upright stride of the tribesman, the pack steady on his back. For all my practice, I cannot match him, and in that there is danger for us all. But it is necessary that I take my share. When Mahmoud, the last of the young men, melted away to join the forces of the Northern Alliance, much of his portion fell to me. I cannot find it in my heart to blame him, for there he will find action, or at least talk.

There is little talk between us now, but it does not leave us silence. The sky is etched with the vapour trails of B52s and the sounds of the bombardments grow daily more constant. It is to the east of us now, fluorescent bursts of light shredding the horizon, and I think of Ghazni, of resting between convoys. Of the smell of oil burning in the flickering lamps as dusk swooped upon us. Of sitting cross-legged around the shiisha, the soft sibilant hubble-bubble lulling us as we passed the pipe from hand to hand. It may be that we will sit there again, but I do not think so. Only the babies cry now when the planes go over, the older children do not even raise their heads.

Without Nazim, they too are rudderless.

He was scooping out the sand for a makeshift well, holding the ragged-edged tin in both hands, when the ground erupted under his fingers, catapulting him through the air. It was Ahmed who ran to him, oblivious of other mines, Ahmed who brought him to safe ground. I ran to my tent and scrabbled around in my belongings for the first aid box and something to ease his pain. I gave him morphine, but it was Ahmed, who, when he felt the boy's limbs go limp, removed the metal from his wounds and stitched them as best he could, Ahmed who laid him gently in his tent.

I knew then, I thought then - who could carry him?

At one in the afternoon, with the noise of bombing echoing in the hills to the north and east, I gave Nazim the last of the morphine and watched his face smooth into sleep. When he woke again at four, Ahmed reached out and touched my arm. I looked up at him. We were thinking the same thing - we had to be - the one donkey, the other children, the snow, which any day now would sweep down from the hills and blanket the valleys, in drifts blown fifteen, twenty feet deep by the strong winter winds. I needed him to say something, to understand, to give consent. I had part-trained him - it could have been me who tripped a land-mine, my 'Ahmed, this is how you use a syringe: always expel a little liquid' an unconscious echo of that other trainer, in that other world, when, clumsy-fingered, I shot a stream of water arching into the air. Now, when I lifted the empty syringe and shook my head, pulling the plunger back, he did not meet my eye, only, without a word, twisted the stick in the binding around Nazim's arm as I had shown him, so that the vein in the elbow bloomed. I waited for a moment, head bowed, then, swallowing the saliva rush in my mouth, flicked my finger twice against the vein, eased the needle into position, and pushed.

It was much easier than I expected. It is much less easy now.

Nazim slipped away quietly, his face pale, but free from pain, and we buried him at sunset, wrapped in the bloodstained blanket, in a shallow grave covered in stones scoured from the hillside. On one, larger and flatter than the rest, Ahmed scratched Nazim al-Haq - Shu Jah - 'brave one' and propped it up at the head. As he rose I put out my hand in a clumsy, foreign gesture, and he touched it briefly, whispering "Shukran", before turning away.

I do not think that I deserve thanks.

In three more days we should make the pass at Zareh Sharan. It may be that they will allow us through - to the border and a measure of hope. Ahmed, his expression carefully blank, moves to the smouldering remains of the fire and begins to rake at it noisily with a stick. The syringe lies in my box, the needle wrapped tightly in cotton-wool. I dare not think that I will use it again. When the fire is dead and the ashes scattered, we shoulder our bundles and move slowly southwards, the women and children straggling after us in a thin line.

Underfoot a pocket of sand shifts and I slip sideways, swallowed ankle-deep. Ahmed reaches out a steadying hand to my elbow, but when I lift my head in thanks his gaze remains fixed on the horizon and he does not turn. And I see that we have both begun this other, more difficult journey, but I cannot tell how it will end.

Only one thing is certain.

The dust blows always from the north and it carries away our footprints in the sand.

Letters (from America, Mostly).

Memphis
15th Aug 1943

Dear Bro,

This is learning to fly all over again! It isn't just us Brits. There are Yanks too, amateurs for the most part, who flew crop dusters and the like before the war. The airstrip lies in the middle of cotton-fields - like a bicycle wheel on its side - a circular landing mat with short strips sticking out all round like spokes. If you don't get into the air fast, you end up nose down in the dirt, bits of cotton lying all along the wings like snow. So far though I'm up. Aerobatics on Monday - spare a thought for me barfing (no prizes for guessing what that means!) into a brown paper bag while hanging upside down at 1500ft.

George.

Dear Uncle Tommy,

What can I tell you about Memphis? - It's *hot!* And not just on the ground - the air is warm right up almost as high as we can fly. The base is surrounded by acres and acres of cotton - the picking's just begun - it's a bit like your tattie-howking, aside from the size of the sacks. It takes a lot of cotton to equal the weight of a bag of potatoes! It isn't all local people either - temporary camps, like mushrooms, have sprung up overnight around every homestead - full of Mexicans and hill-folk mostly. There hasn't been a cloud in the sky since I got here, but I guess farmers are the same the world over - all the talk on a Saturday night is of the possibility of rain coming to spoil the harvest. Everybody works at it, even kids as young as five or six, and old people that look as if they'd fall over under the weight of the sacks. They don't pick Sundays though - they seem to be churchy folk.

Thank Aunt Effie for the muffler, I don't need it yet, but I will,

Regards to all,
George.

Memphis
20th Sept. 1943

Dear Mother,

I trust this finds you well. I'm afraid with training every day we don't get to go to church much, but we do have a 'Bible Joe' from Arkansas who can preach a pretty good sermon, when he's a mind. But you needn't worry, it's not hard to remember your Creator when your plane is in a spin, and you don't know which way is up! Our time here is nearly over and so far I'm doing fine. I'll miss the local children when we move - they sit on their front steps waving as we go over, just like we used to sit on the fence by the cutting at Rathbeg, waiting for a train to pass.

In three weeks I should be in Pensacola. It'll be good to be by the sea again - they say the water's lovely. Bound to be warmer than the Irish Sea anyway.

Your loving son,
George.

Pensacola
1st Oct 1943

Dear Mother,

This is *some* place. You'd *love* the old houses - very elegant, real colonial. Palm trees are everywhere and they *definitely* look better in sunshine! I thought you'd like to see me in my 'ducks'. Unfortunately the building behind me is *not* my billet, though it could be some day - if I get to be a Senior Officer. Our accommodation is not so pretty - we're stationed out of town, in tin huts that rattle in the wind and are about as draughty as one of Uncle Tommy's barns. Speaking of pretty, we had a three day leave and Bud invited me down to his folks in Richmond, Virginia. A cousin of his was getting married. The bride was beautiful (of course) as was Nancy, her bridesmaid. I've been invited to *her* family for my next leave.

Your loving son,
George.

Pensacola
10th Oct 1943

Dear Uncle Tommy,

I guess you're ploughing now. I trust the weather will hold for you. It's still summer here - they have to water the runways to keep them from melting! Sometimes I almost wish for a shower of rain. But they say a Florida storm is something else, and when it does come I'll change my mind.

Regards to Aunt Effie,
George.

Dear Bro,

This has been the best posting yet. The 'field' is just outside of town and we do get *some* time off. Feel for me, lying on the beach under a palm tree, with a bottle of ice-cold beer. And yes, the girls are pretty, and *very* friendly.

George.

Pensacola

20th Oct 1943

Dear Mother,

My training is going well, and I'm enjoying the challenge. I'll find out what section I'm being assigned to soon, though it'll be strange to have to say goodbye to half the lads, when we've been together for so long. In the meantime I'm off to Richmond for a three-day leave and I'm looking forward to seeing Nancy Saar again. Give my best to Uncle Tom and Aunt Effie when you're at the farm.

Your loving son,
George.

Pensacola
10th Nov 1943

Dear Mother,

Thank you for your letter and the photograph. I don't remember the Martin girl, but I'm sure she's very nice and I'm glad she's company for you. But if you could only meet Nancy, I'm sure you'd like her too. I have an open invitation to her folks in Virginia, so I'll be heading there for their Thanksgiving holiday and some "good ol' Southern hospitality". We all crowded round the radio last night to listen to President Roosevelt announce the date - it's been a national holiday here since 1789 - the Yanks sure know how to cheer.

Your loving son,
George.

Richmond
26th Nov 1943

Dear Uncle Tommy,

Thanksgiving's a bit like Harvest Festival and Christmas rolled into one. And what a turkey! You'd have been proud to have bred it. I felt almost guilty tucking in, thinking of you folks on rations, but I guess I'll be on shorter rations myself soon enough. We all just want to get on with it now and have our pop at Jerry, before it's all over.

Regards to Aunt Effie,
George.

Pensacola
10th Dec 1943

Dear Bro,

What's this I hear about a 'young lady' - is it serious? Mother said - but I guess you'll know what mother said! I take it she's got brains, as you met her in college, but I hope she's pretty, and not *too* much of a blue-stocking. Speaking of stockings - maybe the enclosed will help you along a bit, the girls here just can't imagine painting seam lines down the back of their legs! Do they get them straight?

Keep me posted,
George.

Pensacola
20th Dec 1943

Dear Mother,

By the time you get this I'll be in Richmond for Christmas. It's my last leave before final training. I've enclosed a photograph of Nancy - I do wish you could meet her - she's *quite* a girl. Beautiful and funny and with a gift for making me forget just why we're here. If you look *very* carefully you may make out her hat.

With best wishes for the festive season, your loving son,
George.

Richmond
26th Dec 1943

Dear Mother,

Nancy and I are engaged! We're hoping to get married in March. You might think it a little soon, but I'll be posted by the summer, and after that, who knows? Her parents have a vacant lot down by the river, so we're going to build our own house. And there'll be a job waiting for me in her father's engineering works when this is all over.

I wish you could be here for the wedding, but I know you'll give us your blessing.

With much love from me, and the future Mrs. Wright,
George.

Pensacola
20th Jan 1944

Dear Mother,

We're in the final stages of our training and have very little spare time, but I wanted to ask you to thank Mr Edgar for his kind offer, but I don't see myself running a shop. I like it here. And if you could only see it I think you would too. I'll write again as soon as I'm able, in the meantime Nancy's folks send their best regards,

Much love from us both,
George.

Dear Bro,

I'm in!!! We move to Maine on Thursday for fighter training. I thought sure I was headed for Bomber Command after being grounded last week for 'buzzing' a bridge. We were aiming to get our whole section home under the radar, and there it was and worth $2 to me, so I just *had* to do it. Eck says that's what swung it. Taffy and Bud and Alec are in too, but Clive and Ronnie are headed for the Great Lakes. I *won't* miss the smell of Ronnie's feet.

Fighter squadron here I come,
George.

Richmond,
24th Mar 1944

Dear Bro,

Tomorrow I'll be married and Miami-bound. We'll be staying at the Tatem Surf Club - I want to give Nancy a real good time - we only have five days.

George.

Miami
26th Mar 1944

Dear Mother,

I wish you could all have been here to see us married. I know you would have approved of the service - the pastor took 1st Corinthians 13 as his text. It won't be hard to keep to it with Nancy as my wife. I'll send a photograph of the wedding as soon as I can.

Nancy hopes it won't be too long before she can meet you,

Much love from us both,
George.

Lewiston,
2nd Apr 1944

Dear Bro,

A job, a house and a wife! Never pictured you as a country school-master, but I guess you've changed some. We're due home leave before we go East, so I hope to see you all then, but don't hold your breath. If not, maybe this'll all be over in time for your first christening - unless there's something you haven't told me. I'm looking forward to meeting Anne,

George.

Lewiston,
23rd Apr 1944

Dear Bro,

Did mother get the wedding photo I sent? Her last letter didn't mention it. I thought you'd appreciate this one, but you'd best keep it to yourself - it's the remains of my latest Martlet - No. 6!! now residing in Lewiston graveyard. The undercarriage, wings and tail unit were carried away by three separate trees. It gave me an excuse to have recuperation leave.

Guess where I went?
George.

Lewiston,
14th June 1944

Dear Bro,

I'm just back from a day at Bar Harbour. The Holloways, with typical American generosity, keep open house for us airmen. What a place! Swimming pool, tennis court, ballroom, and the longest dining table you've ever seen. They aren't fussy about how you hold your cutlery though. (Thank goodness.) I sent another photograph to mother - has she mentioned it?

All the best for your job - forty children to control isn't my idea of fun!

George.

Lewiston,
2nd July 1944

Dear Bro,

This is finally it. I've been posted - 1851 Fleet Fighter Squadron. I can't help feeling proud, though I'm not sure that mother feels the same way, for she hasn't replied to my last letter. I'll be joining the carrier at Edenderry, so should manage to see her then. Before that I have one week in Richmond. My last chance to experience an American holiday - they sure know how to party. I wish I could bring Nancy over in September, I'm sure if mother met her she'd feel differently.

Taffy and Bud died in a mid-air collision yesterday. What a waste. I hope, if I buy it, that I take an enemy out with me.

See you soon,
George.

HMS Gannet,
1st Oct 1944

Dear Mother,

We're headed out and I don't expect any more leave before it's all over. When it is, and Nancy and I are settled in Richmond, I hope you'll re-consider and come out to spent some time with us. I know you'd love her if you just gave yourself a chance and her folks have been real kind to me.

Your loving son,
George.

Richmond,
Oct 30th 1944

Dear Mrs Wright,

I wanted you to be the first to know, after George of course, though I'm not sure when he'll get my letter. I'm going to have a baby - it's due next April, and I'm so excited. I don't mind if it's a boy or a girl just so long as it's healthy.

With fondest regards,
Nancy Morgan Wright.

Richmond

March 20th 1945

Dear Mrs Wright,

I guess you didn't get my first letter. I hope
you get this one. You have a beautiful grandson.
He's a mite small on account of being early, but I
just know he'll grow up fine and straight, like his
daddy. They say the war in Europe'll soon be
over, so maybe you can get to meet him real soon.
I sure hope so.

May I call you 'Mom'?

Yours, lovingly,
Nancy Morgan Wright.

Telegram, from Admiralty House
to Nancy Morgan Wright,
Sleepy Hollow, Richmond, Virginia, USA.
We regret to inform you that Sub-lieutenant (A)
George Arthur Wright, H.M.S. Gannet, died in
active service on 20th March 1945.

Richmond,
April 14th 1945

Dear Mrs Wright,

I am so sorry to be sending you this news, but I received the enclosed telegram today. I still find it hard to believe that my darling George is gone - and on the very same day that George Junior was born. I wish I knew how or where, but I guess that's all they can say just now. I miss him so much and I know you will too, so just as soon as I'm able, I'd like to come spend some time with you. It won't be the same without George, but I know he'd want me to come just the same. In the meantime, I'm enclosing a photograph of George Junior. Isn't he just beautiful?

Please write soon,

Yours lovingly,
Nancy Morgan Wright.

Richmond,
May 8th 1945

Dear Mrs Wright,

I wanted to write you tonight because I guess we'll be feeling the same thing. Of course I'm glad the war in Europe is over, but I can't celebrate with everyone else. It is just the cruellest thing to have lost George when he so nearly made it through. Little Georgie is doing fine though, and every day I thank the Lord for him. I'm looking forward to introducing him to his Irish Grandma. I expect the post hasn't been reliable before, but I hope to hear from you soon now,

Yours lovingly,
Nancy Morgan Wright.

Richmond
4rd July 1945

Dear Mrs Wright,

I hope that you are well. I thought the post would have been better by now, but Maw says I just need to be patient. It's hard though when all I want is to finally meet you. I've been thinking about George so much today - this time last year he was here, and if he hadn't had that last leave I wouldn't have little Georgie now. Holding him helps me so much - I know it would you too. They say that travel to Europe will be possible by the autumn, so I'm saving hard for a ticket and we'll be on that first boat.

Lovingly yours,
Nancy Morgan Wright.

Derryboy,
4th August 1945

Dear Mother,

I appreciate it must be lonely for you in Bangor on your own, and difficult too, with all the memories of George, so of course Anne and I would be happy for you to come here to live with us. It is odd though that you haven't heard anything from Nancy. And fortunate that you were notified by the Admiralty - maybe George requested that. You don't think... no, I'm sure Nancy must have been notified too. Anne says she's very young and perhaps with George gone she just wants to start again. But not even to write - from what he said of her she didn't seem that kind of girl. I keep thinking maybe a letter has gone astray somehow. Don't you think you should ask the solicitor to arrange that if anything comes after you move it can be sent on? I don't know what size Richmond is - perhaps I could try to trace her folks. We'll come down next weekend to help you start sorting the house - maybe something will turn up then,

Much love,
John and Anne.

Battenberg for Tea

The envelope in her hands was long and slim, the paper crisp. In the left-hand corner the scrolled letterhead stood out - deep burgundy against cream. Jean reached for the paper-knife, but startled by the one-o'clock gun, it slipped from her fingers and fell through the narrow gap between the sideboard and the bookcase. She set the letter down - it would keep. Anyway she was late.

The air was damp and cold. Jean emerged from the close and headed down the High Street. She bent her head against the thin wind which slanted the rain into her face in sharp, stinging flurries. If she didn't hurry the tables might be full and she would have to wait. She hated waiting. Waiting meant being squeezed into the narrow hallway, pressed against other bodies. It meant breathing in stale breath and the mingled odours of damp clothes and sweat and smoke. It meant being nervous and uncomfortable and sometimes unaccountably afraid.

In the doorway she paused to remove her rain-mate, jerking the ties so that the water spurted off, landing in a spatter of drops on the pavement, merging into the dampness. Peering through the steamy glass in the door she noted, with relief, the empty umbrella stand and clear passageway - the weather must be keeping some folk at home. She pushed open the outer door and edged through the gap, shutting it carefully behind her, but the draught from the street still caught the inner door, swinging it wide. With a smile of apology for the couple sitting nearest to it she made for a table in the corner set for four.

Jean preferred to sit at a table for four, for sharing with just one other person was awkward, especially if it was a man. She had to make sure that her leg or knee or foot didn't accidentally brush against his under the table, and if it did... even the thought made her blush with embarrassment. But with three, or better still two others, she could feel safe. They would talk to each other and she could sit quietly, with her meal and her thoughts, and only the occasional momentary contact of passing the salt or water.

Today's 'Special' was Macaroni Cheese. She ate slowly, allowing the heat in the room to percolate through her, to begin to dry off her stockings and old, once-sturdy brogues. As usual, she took her tea afterwards, with a plain biscuit, to assuage her guilt at not vacating her place. Sometimes, near the beginning of the month, she took a warmed pancake with lemon juice and sugar, or a scone with butter and jam. The scones were particularly good, light and crumbly, reminding her of the old days, when she sat at a window table in Jenner's restaurant, high above Princes Street, with Morag, Lillian and Catherine. They would discuss 'The Bostonians' and 'Madame Bovary' over a leisurely cream tea, looking out towards the gardens, the Art Gallery, the Scott Monument and the Castle.

Things were different now, her meagre stocks and shares dwindling and her pension losing value steadily as interest rates fell. She needed to eat cheaply, to save on gas, to store up warmth, paid for by someone else. Eating out had been reduced from a pleasureable 'occasion' to an economy measure, forced on her by diminished circumstances. She hadn't been brought up to grumble, but it was nice sometimes to pretend. Especially today, with the knowledge of the unopened letter on her sideboard pressing heavily on her.

Nice too to pretend that she was young again. To roll back the years and see herself slight and straight, joints mobile, hearing clear.

– Lunchtimes on Salisbury Crags: a clutch of Miss Marchmont's secretaries strung out like a long line of paper dolls, angled against the wind, laughing as they were gusted backwards, skirts whipping around their legs, revealing flashes of ankle and stocking and neat buttoned boot. She could still feel her hair lifted and tugged from confining pins, unruly curls rioting around her face.

– Summer evenings in the Botanics: the rules of the game simple and well-defined. Young women clustered on the grass, elegant knots of pleat and ruffle in pink and lilac and cream; young men strolling self-consciously past in twos or threes, making a show of earnest discussion. The women's heads bent close together as they whispered comments and critiques behind their gloved hands and shafted glances of admiration or dismissal, obliquely, from under the wide shadows of their hats.

– And perhaps best of all, the long Sunday afternoons, coiled into an armchair reading Scott and Stevenson; without glasses, without the print blurring, without a headache.

The girl stopped by the table and set down the folded bill. "No hurry."

Jean glanced upwards, smiling automatically, still abstracted. "Thank you, my dear." She was never sure if the girl meant what she said, or if it was a polite way to move folk on. Nevertheless, she moved to get up, flexing to relieve the stiffness in her knee and the dull, arthritic ache in her left shoulder. Buttoning her coat she turned towards the window. Slanting rain still bounced against the glass, sliding downwards in thin, continuous lines. She opened her rain-mate and set it neatly over her hat, tying the ends firmly under her chin.

Out on the street she shivered against the wind and turned to trudge back up the hill. Home, she hung her coat to drip over the bath and draped the rain-mate, open, on the cold tap. In the living room she peeled off her stockings, rolling each leg neatly to the knee before sitting down and continuing, resting her feet on a pouffe to avoid having to bend too far. She chafed them with a towel until pink colour began to creep back into her toes - it was a matter of pride that her feet were still slim and straight, not needing the ministrations of a chiropodist - the product of a lifetime of sensible shoes. But, as always, she felt a pang of regret as she hid them in her thick, woollen 'house' tights and faded slippers. As she reached for the coat that, though seated and frayed around the cuffs and neck, was still thick enough to provide warmth, the letter caught her eye. Beside it, a photograph in an embossed silver frame. Two young women, laughing into the camera lens. Two young men, lounging at their feet, the braid, even in black and white, standing out proudly around their cuffs. In front of them the remnants of their afternoon tea spread out on a rug. Andrew had drawn a circle around the Battenberg cake and scrawled a caption under it: 'Lill's favourite'. They had all meant to grow old together. She stared at the picture, her brow puckered. Someone recently had reminded her of Lillian.

She shook her head, picked up the letter - there was no point in delaying any further. Once a letter from her lawyer had been commonplace, the regular statement of a healthy portfolio, which she had scanned briefly, content to note the final figure, before filing it carefully in her desk. But that had been before Fred Goodwin and the banking crash. Now she faced the quarterly communications with ever-increasing dread. He wanted to see her. There were some matters that needed to be discussed. He suggested a time, if it wasn't suitable could she phone to make an alternative appointment. Her mouth curved into a wry smile. In the pattern of her days any time was suitable. He knew that. But she appreciated the polite fiction that gave her time importance.

*   *   *

Jean perched, sparrow-like, on the edge of the chair in the waiting room, rocking forward a fraction so that her feet rested on the floor. Her hands were tightly clasped, the knuckles showing white. Like all waiting rooms it was featureless, devoid of character, impersonal. The walls were variously decorated with copies of a 'Legal Liability' Insurance certificate, the Law Society Membership of the numerous partners, and the obligatory mock-oil 'Constable' in a heavy gilt-coloured frame. Leaflets on a side table proclaimed the firm's expertise in conveyancing, divorce, death. She supposed they would deal with hers, when the time came, with a bored, routine efficiency: the thought no longer troubling her. Her will was three pages of unintelligible 'lawyerese', which had always seemed to Jean a very long-winded way to disperse what little remained of her estate to good causes in which she still took an interest. If it wasn't all swallowed in fees.

The lawyer's office was light and spacious. It was the first time that Jean had been in this particular room and she noticed with appreciation the highly polished sheen on the mahogany table which dominated the centre of the room and the tall, breakfront bookcase that filled one wall.

The lawyer nodded. "Mrs Greer, please…" he pulled out a chair, and with no apparent effort slid her in towards the table. Piles of papers were spread out in front of him and he rested his wrists on them, tapping the tips of his fingers together as he talked. He passed a sheet over to her and she tried to concentrate on his involved explanations of the figures. The basis of what he said was clear, but the details eluded her, the print dancing before her eyes. Without her glasses it was hopeless. Sunlight, pouring in through the long windows, coloured her cheeks and she felt her eyelids grow heavy, her attention drifting as his voice faded into the background drone of traffic. She sat up straighter, forcing herself to focus; as he summarized her situation, the words dropping into her mind like stones, the implications rippling outwards, lapping at the edges of her brain.

"You do see…" His voice was practised, simultaneously stern and sympathetic, "…the necessity of what I'm saying?"

"Oh yes… yes. It's just… I don't quite know…" She was looking past him, her eyes fixed on the windows overlooking the crescent. From the central garden the sound of a gate creaking on un-oiled hinges floated upwards. Once she too had held a key to a crescent garden. She met his eyes. "I don't quite know if it would *do.*"

*   *   *

'Lodger' The word made her uncomfortable, much like the phrase 'Self-Aid Society' on the labels in the dimly-lit shop where she placed her cross-stitch bookmarks. She thought them attractive, and requiring little in the way of materials, had dreamed of the profit she would make, but it seemed few folk read real books anymore, or if they did, were happy to turn down the corner of a page. She considered her living room: the trolley by her chair, a plastic flask of hot water saved from breakfast sitting on the embroidered tray-cloth, and the contrasting dainty silver tea-pot and fragile, scalloped cup and saucer. She could no longer afford pride, but a lodger? Try as she might she couldn't visualise another person a permanent presence here. She had grown old alone, those friends that had survived that early, shocking flurry falling, like spiraling leaves, one by one, until privacy had become a protective shell she was almost afraid to break. It would be nice though not to have to scrimp and save, or to have her every movement defined by small, spirit-sapping economies. The scales tipped and tilted in her mind - privacy versus poverty, mere existence versus comfort. Tomorrow she would have one last check at the shop. There was talk on the radio about a renaissance of interest in old-fashioned things - 'retro' they called it. If her bookmarks had become retro, perhaps she could expand her range and make cards too.

A lone piper played outside the Royal Academy as Jean crossed Princes Street. She wondered, not for the first time, if the council paid him? Or if he stood there, day after day, in the wind and rain of Edinburgh's unpredictable summer, trusting in the few pennies that tourists dropped in the tray at his feet. Perhaps he lodged with someone. Just supposing she decided… would she get someone like that? For an instant she imagined him practicing his pipes in the small back bedroom, the sound reverberating round the close. She couldn't help but smile. That would definitely *not* do. None of her bookmarks were in the shop window and, hope rising, she went inside. The lady at the counter looked up with a smile that faded when she recognized Jean, the fractional shake of her head enough. There was no other way.

She decided to go straight to the café for lunch, and though it was hardly an occasion for celebration, ordered the 'roast of the day', to the obvious surprise of the waitress. In the brief lull between coffees and lunches she heard snatches of conversation as the girls cleared the tables. She didn't intend to listen - it was impolite to eavesdrop; but when she heard the words 'leave the flat' and 'end of the month' her mouth went dry. She ordered a second cup of tea to give herself time to think. How would one ask? Each time the girl passed by the table Jean lifted her head only to lower it again. The likeness to Lillian was really quite uncanny. On the far wall a noticeboard was studded with small cards advertising everything from 'bikes for sale' to 'situations vacant'. That was the answer. Her hand trembled as she filled out the card: 'Room available, shared kitchen and bathroom, Royal Mile.'

*   *   *

As Lorna stepped into the echoing stairwell, Jean, who had come out onto the landing to meet her when she heard the jangle of the bell, saw her shiver and was glad that she'd put on the gas fire to take the chill from the flat. Glad too that she'd dusted the urn of dried grasses that stood at the turn of the stair, and removed the cobwebs from the fluted metal ribs that supported the handrail. In the month since it had been arranged that Lorna would take the room, Jean had dusted and polished until the flat shone, the scent of lavender filling every room. And as she did so, she thought more and more of Andrew and Johnnie, of Lillian.

Memories, submerged for years, surfaced in her mind, rolling over her like waves, swelling and surging, breaking and receding, leaving behind a surf of images, tangled, glistening. At first she had been able to skim them off, one by one, separating them, sharpening, bringing them into focus. But as the past became vividly alive, the present blurred. Images of Lorna and Lillian, superimposed, began to merge. She tried hard to keep them distinct, to distinguish between then and now, but gradually she allowed time to slip imperceptibly into a single sequence, without chronology. She struggled to remember why it was that Lillian had stayed away so long, why Johnnie and Andrew weren't here to welcome her home; perhaps they'd come soon. Everything was ready. The small table was set in the parlour to catch the last of the sunshine, and the kettle on the hob was just beginning to sing. It would be good to be together again. And there was a Battenberg for tea.

Magda's War

October 1915: Karl.

Magda is kneeling by the hearth, holding a third match to the paper crumpled under a wigwam of kindling. A rush of air behind her lifts the wisps of hair at the base of her neck, fans the fire into flame. She rocks back onto her heels, pivots to face the door. Karl is framed in the entrance as if sprung from one of the photographs lined up along the mantle-shelf: awkward in ill-fitting grey serge and long boots, a spiked helmet clutched against his chest.

She has faced this moment three times already, spreads her hands in denial.

"I must, Mutti," he says, pride and defiance in his voice.

*   *   *

July 1914: Johann.

The talk is everywhere: of the noble Prussian cause, of the defence of the Fatherland, of honour and duty and sacrifice and pride. Crushed into the flag-waving, foot-stamping crowd that throngs the square, Magda listens to the Burgermeister calling on the men of the town, thrills to his voice. People are leaning from the windows of the half-timbered houses, while from the doorways squat matrons encourage their menfolk forward, stirred by the playing of the band, by patriotic fervour, by an irresistible urge to have a part in this. Beside her Johann, chest swelling, his deep baritone blending with the music, the 'Heil Dir im Siegerkranz' - 'Hail to Thee in Victor's Crown' - welling up in her also. Amid cheers, he is the first to step forward, the first to be swallowed by the press in the doorway of the town hall, the first to re-emerge with his papers stamped, his head held high. She already sees a medal nestling in the velvet blue of its case beside the photograph that she will commission from Herr Mencken before Johann leaves. She thinks of the carved frame in the photographer's window, calculates the money hidden in the rust-edged treacle tin. It will be enough.

As they thrust their way homewards through the crowd she clings to his arm, smiling up at him, taking two steps to his one, pride in her eyes. Everyone they pass nods approval and each time someone claps him on the shoulder he seems to grow taller, more erect. She wants to ask "When?"

and "For how long?" but determines to wait for the privacy of their kitchen - it is enough for now that he leads the way.

Their farm is on the edge of town, not far from Frau Weber's cottage. As they pass Magda sees the curtain waver, feels Johann's grip on her arm tighten, drops her head. She has not seen Frau Weber since Herr Weber's outburst in church and Magda misses their weekly gossip over coffee and streusselkuchen. But Johann has remained adamant - for who can risk the taint of cowardice.

Magda polishes Johann's belt buckle until she sees her reflection shimmering on the surface. She thinks of it imprinted there, always with him, along with the lock of hair he has secreted in a slip of paper folded into his tunic pocket. At the station she clings to him, decorum forgotten, their final kiss indistinguishable from the many others in the maelstrom of bodies thronging the platform. Then the scramble to board, doors slamming, a flurry of handkerchiefs, the blur of Johann's face behind the grimy glass, as the train disappears in clouds of steam. His last promise - to write every week - warms her, lessens her loss. Beside her the boys, each with their own, clearly-voiced regrets: Rudi and Tomas that they are six months too young, Karl that it will all be over before he has even a chance to serve.

A letter comes, stray fragments of phrases remaining amongst the blacked-out lines. '…all well…' '…home for Christmas…' '…always in my prayers.'

She touches it to her face, seeking the strong, warm smell of him, finds instead an acrid sharpness, troubling in its unfamiliarity.

A second letter, less intelligible than the first, the odour of infection and old blood faint, but unmistakable. A third so disjointed that she is almost glad when a pre-printed postcard comes instead. She devours the one remaining sentence, 'I am wounded, but not seriously.' as if it were good news.

"As it is," insists Herr Gruber, the Werbeoffizier, when she proffers it at church, seeking his opinion - who better to ask than the recruiting officer?

His voice is authoritative, his words plausible, though spoken as if by rote. "There are rest areas behind the lines, where those with minor injuries can recuperate. These cards are sent from there. He will be recovered soon."

She needs to believe him and so suppresses her doubts, nods her thanks. But as she turns to leave, his hand lingers a fraction too long on her arm, a hint of implication in his eyes,

"If I can be of help… do not hesitate to ask."

There are two more postcards. On the last, the remaining sentence reads: 'I am well.' She takes it to church tucked inside her prayer book, reads it a dozen times during the service, her relief spilling over into a smile for Herr Gruber on the way out.

*   *   *

It has been six months now, the Schlieffen Plan all but forgotten, and in the town a handful of men trickle home, their physical injuries obvious, their other problems less so. Magda seeks one out - a casual labourer who worked for them at harvest-time. She is eager for news of Johann, but he barely lifts his head when she enters, remaining hunched over the scullery fire, his greatcoat tightly buttoned, mumbling to himself. His hands lie on his lap, their constant tremor punctuated by an intermittent, involuntary jerk of his head.

His wife kneels in front of him, takes one hand in hers, speaks slowly as if to a child, "Berthold, do you have any news of Herr Hoffmann?"

He puckers his forehead as if the question is too hard for him, then covers his ears with his hands, shaking his head from side to side.

Magda has been using old wool to knit socks for the boys and has brought him a pair also. She sets them on his knee and he snatches at them, pulling them onto his hands before thrusting them behind his back.

His wife touches his shoulder, says, "No one here will steal them, Berthold." When she fails to get a response she shakes her head at Magda, offering thanks and an apology. "That was kind of you. I'm sorry that he cannot help."

In the hearth the flames leap, yet despite the grubby greatcoat he shivers.

Magda, seeking understanding, questions, "He cannot be cold?"

"Not cold. But…" There is no bitterness in his wife's voice, only a sadness that tears at Magda. "The tremor never leaves him, awake or asleep." Her words pour out as if a burden released, "Asleep is worse, for in his sleep he cries." She brushes at the single tear sliding down the side of her nose, looks past Magda to the darkening sky. "No matter what I do or say, it's as if he's not really here."

*   *   *

January 1915: Rudi.

Frost silvers the ground, the furrows set like stone, when Rudi appears with his papers, unruly hair tamed, his uniform a loosely tied brown paper parcel under his arm. Magda forces herself to smile, calls him "My brave boy." But after he too has gone, spirited away on the troop train heading for Brussels, Tomas, whose work in the munitions factory is reckoned essential, prowls about the house like a caged lion, so that a coldness clutches at her breast. There has not been a postcard from Johann for some months now and she clings to Rudi's promise that he will send news.

Herr Gruber, when she asks, says, "You must understand, the divisions are constantly on the move, and to send word home often difficult. Johann's name has not appeared in the lists?" When she shakes her head, he dismisses her fears. "Then you have nothing to worry about... trust me."

She is aware of his eyes fixed on her, of his voice, chocolate-smooth.

"With Tomas in the factory and Rudi gone, you will be short-handed on the farm. I too am strong... and willing."

She has no desire to be rude, but nor will she encourage him, for when this is over she wants to be able to hold to Johann without restraint, without any regrets. And besides, she is not one of those wives who find loneliness too great a struggle and must take solace elsewhere; who are talked about in whispers; who are stared at in the street, but not spoken to.

*   *   *

June 1915: Tomas.

The war is almost a year old and the chemists in Tomas' factory have developed a new weapon: one that will end the conflict, and quickly. He cannot talk of it, but a pride that he has played his part fizzes in him. Magda knows where Johann and Rudi are now, or at least where they have been - the unfamiliar names that have become common knowledge in the town stamped on her heart - Zandvoorde, Gheluvelt, Langemarck. Herr Gruber catches her eye as she leaves the church, hurries to greet her, the hand that grips hers hot, slicked with sweat. He confirms that the Fourth Army is holding a line at Ypres; that word may come soon.

It isn't word that comes, but Rudi. She reaches up to embrace him, senses him shrinking back, sees his mouth working.

56

"I'm sorry, Mutti."

Later, in the flickering firelight, his face in shadow, he talks to her: of comradeship and bravery, of how his father ran out under fire to bring back a lad fallen in his first action. He does *not* talk of the sights and sounds that fill his night terrors, robbing him of sleep. Of the lice and the rats and sucking mud, of constant artillery fire, the bursting of shells and the raw, unending damp. Or of his father's last weaving run, not towards the enemy, but away from them; of how he was dragged back from behind their own lines, to die, blindfolded, at dawn.

To Tomas, Rudi says only, "Stay. Work in the factory. Look after Mutti. There will be few of us come home. Fewer still fit for anything when we do."

But when Rudi leaves two days later, Tomas goes also. Volunteering in a detachment carrying the new weapon to the German front. Proud that he can heft the gas canisters with ease, he flexes his muscles, jokes, "If I had not been a farmboy…"

This time when the train leaves Magda cannot contain her tears. And afterwards, Sunday-by-Sunday she flushes under Herr Gruber's gaze, wishes herself invisible.

September 1915: Karl.

Karl has taken Tomas' place in the factory. "For the meantime, Mutti."

Magda, understanding what Karl has not said, prays for time to slow, for the war to be over. When she allows herself to think of Johann, it is as if she teeters on the edge of a chasm, from which, if she were to fall, there would be no return. She focuses on her absent sons, praying nightly over their photographs, and on Karl, her prayers seasoning every meal she cooks for him, ironed into his clothes.

Herr Gruber sits opposite her in church now, rising as she enters, bowing her into her seat. Week by week he contrives to join her as they leave, enquiring as to her health, the farm; reminding her always, "You have only to ask."

The news from the front is of progress made, of the success of the new gas, that victory is only a matter of time. Yet rumours persist: that those in command are preparing for another winter; that the gas causes many casualties amongst their own men also. When Magda questions Karl he is dismissive, insistent.

"It's all nonsense, Mutti - enemy propaganda."

She would like to believe him, but he fails to meet her eyes.

The lists of the dead are posted weekly on the noticeboard outside the town hall and each Monday Magda joins the press of women clustered around it, her shoulders tight as she scans the names. On the day that Tomas' name appears she collapses against the door, many hands helping her inside. Herr Gruber brings a chair, a glass of water; hovers over her.

She manages a 'Danke Schon', unaware that she has agreed that he may help her home. Handing her down from the cart he offers to stay until Karl returns, but she shakes her head. "I think I'll rest now."

His expression slides from solicitous to an irritation, quickly masked, and he pounces on her involuntary shiver, "I'll light the fire for you. Where is your kindling?"

She shakes her head again, more definite this time, "Danke, but no. I am better alone."

Now it is Johann and Tomas both that inhabit her dreams: lifeless statues carved of her grief. And beyond them Rudi: shadowy, grotesque; hunched over a folding table, writing endless messages on scraps of paper that crumble to dust as she strains to grasp them. A single postcard, all that came of his promise, is propped against the tobacco tin on the kitchen windowsill, the edges curling.

*   *   *

October 1915: Karl.

Since Tomas' death it is as if Karl too is hovering on the edge of her life, a fledgling poised for flight. His eighteenth birthday is barely a month away, the jumper she is knitting for him a match for the one she has just finished for Rudi, for surely they will all be home soon. It is Monday, but today she cannot face the lists and so remains at home to finish her knitting instead.

There is a knock at the door, Herr Gruber standing outside. "You weren't in town today. I came to see that you are all right?"

'I'm very busy.' And then, not wishing to sound rude, she offers, "But I appreciate your concern." She moves forward to shut the door, his foot remaining on the step signalling his intention.

"Frau Hoffmann…"

She can guess what's coming, doesn't wish to hear it. "Herr Gruber." She inclines her head, "I'm sorry, but I have something I must finish before Karl comes home."

He steps back as courtesy demands and she shuts the door before he changes his mind, sliding down to sit with her back against it lest he attempt to force his way in. Perhaps she won't go to church this Sunday.

The light is failing as she casts off the last sleeve of Karl's jumper and laying it aside kneels to put a match to the fire. Behind her a rush of air.

She turns and sees Karl in the doorway, the uniform ill-fitting, the spiked helmet crushed against his chest. "No. No!"

He is looking above her, to the mantle-shelf, his "I must Mutti," sharp as a bayonet thrust. And then, as if he reads her mind, he offers, "It is my duty."

She shakes her head, dismissing the propaganda, thinks instead of Frau Rilke: losing both her sons on one day; of Hans Kiefer: shuffling through the town square, his sleeve pinned at his shoulder, one side of his face a ploughed field.

Karl takes a conciliatory step towards her, indicates the discarded knitting, his voice breaking, "I'll need this... I can take Rudi's also." He holds his head high, "I *want* to go, Mutti."

Her thoughts fly: to the box under the bed with the bundle of birth certificates tied in once-purple ribbon, the ink of the dates and place of birth similarly faded. To Herr Gruber and his position as Werbeoffizier, his hitherto unwanted advances.

"When?" she asks, injecting strength into her voice.

"On the next troop train, a week maybe."

"You'll stay in the factory until you go?"

Karl sets down the helmet to touch her arm, nods as if relieved that she makes no protest. "There is so much to do…"

She captures his hand, tries, "You are useful *here*."

His voice has a new firmness: youth replaced by a forced manhood. "I am needed *there*. We all are."

She cannot look at him dressed as he is, so searches for a reason for him to remove the uniform, to be as he was before. "For your father and brothers, I sewed on names… I'll do the same for you."

In the morning, once Karl leaves for the factory, Magda fetches the box. She lays his birth certificate on the table under the window, weighing it down with a knife at each corner. The lettering, though pale, is elegant, the numbering also - it will not be so easy to make a seven into an eight. For a moment she thinks of making his birthdate 1899 instead, but though it would be simpler to do, it is too much of a risk. And surely the war cannot last more than another year. Casting about for something to practice on she takes the sharpest of her knives and removes the end paper from her prayer book. Herr Gruber will know the truth, but there are other eyes she may need to deceive. The new '8' she allows to dry naturally, not daring to blot the thinned ink lest the original is exposed.

At the town hall she hovers in the background until there is a lull in the line of boys queuing at the Werbeoffizier's desk. Outside in the square, the band's rendition of the recruitment hymn is more vigorous than ever, and she steels herself against the lie. Herr Gruber continues writing as she approaches the table, speaks without raising his head. "Sitzen Sie." She pulls back the chair, and perhaps alerted by the rustle of her skirt he looks up, his pupils darkening as he rises. He rises, bows over her hand. "Frau Hoffmann. An unexpected pleasure." He gestures to the chair, "Bitte."

She unfolds the birth certificate, lays it out before him.

He looks at it for a long moment before meeting her gaze. "I see." His finger traces the date, halts at the year. "I understand your feelings but there are certain... difficulties."

She leans forward, her hands clasped. "If he is only seventeen…"

"Indeed, but he has already signed. Have you thought of how he will react, whether he will contradict you?"

"I thought," she looks down at the certificate, the numbers blurring, "That if the factory were to need him here, were to refuse to let him go… that perhaps he need not know."

Herr Gruber's hand covers hers and she swallows.

"And you have come to me?"

"You have influence."

"Perhaps." He glances around as if to give credence to his words. "But this is not something to discuss here." His tongue flicks over his lips. "If you would be so good as to call at my house…" He leaves the sentence hanging, increases the pressure on her fingers.

Behind Magda someone coughs and Herr Gruber removes his hand, becomes brisk. "I will look into it. Good-day, Frau Hoffmann."

Karl is working late at the factory. It is only a short walk to Herr Gruber's house in the growing dusk. Magda pauses at the gate and for a fraction of a second wonders if she has been mistaken; but the memory of his eyes devouring her is too strong. Light shines from an oil lamp in the kitchen, and as Herr Gruber passes the window his shadow is cast along the path: predatory, huge. She cannot do it.

The following evening and the next, while Karl is at work, she dresses carefully, makes her way out of town towards Herr Gruber's house; each time failing to get past the gate.

On the fourth day Karl comes home at lunchtime, his eyes shining. He grips Magda by the shoulders, excitement spilling, "The troop train is expected any day now, I may be very late tonight."

When he leaves again for the factory his words remain, stamped on every surface, taunting her wherever she turns. She lights the fire under the copper, drags the tin bath from the alcove. As she fills it, the enormity of what she has done, what she thinks to do, presses upon her, a weight impossible to shift. Yet did not even Christ say, *'Let him that is without sin cast the first stone.'* She clutches at the thought - perhaps *he* would not condemn her.

Dried lavender hangs in a muslin bag in her wardrobe and she sprinkles the flower heads onto the steaming water, the rising scent releasing her tension, strengthening her resolve.

The track to Herr Gruber's house is a nave, whisper-quiet, the arch of trees above transforming it into an ever-changing mosaic of light and shade. In her head the litany: '*Lord have mercy, Christ have mercy...*' Afternoon heat is bleeding out of the sun as she reaches his gate and she thrusts it aside, not allowing herself to pause. At the end of the path a shallow flight of steps rises towards the door, and for a moment she is in church, at the foot of the steps leading to the high altar, the cross above glittering in the flicker of candlelight. She shakes her head to dispel the image, and before she can change her mind raps on the door. As it opens she is thinking of Johann: his grave forever hidden from her; of Tomas: killed by the gas he helped to produce; of Rudi: the lack of news chilling. Preceding Herr Gruber down the passageway, she feels the heat of his hand in the small of her back, the increasing hammer-beat of her heart. She shuts her eyes, slows her breathing, floods her mind with Karl.

Gulls Calling

The letter came on the first of July. In the narrow hallway Agnes turned the envelope over and over in her hand. It was official, franked. There had been talk, oh, ages before, when the men from the council came, looking around, asking questions. Talk of hot water and bathrooms and such-like. And raised rents. Agnes had been both sceptical and undisturbed. "This'll do me my day", she told them. They had nodded and mumbled non-committally, perhaps reasoning that at eighty-seven 'her day' might not be very long.

Now, standing in the scullery, leaning against the washer for support, the words twisted like a knot in her stomach. She had not expected this. The knob handle of the mangle was pressing into the small of her back and she was aware of a dull ache but could not pin-point its cause. She shifted uneasily. Fancy it coming today... the beginning of the marching season.

Doors were opening up and down the street. She could hear a confused babble of voices. People clustered in groups, letters fluttering in their hands like huge white butterflies. Voices mingled: strident, conciliatory, excited, protesting. Big Johnnie, loud and angry. All mouth, thought Agnes, he'll be the first to go.

All day Agnes stayed inside, her door firmly shut. Once or twice she heard footsteps and a half-hesitant knocking. But she remained anchored to her chair in the back room. She wanted to think. In this, as in everything, she would make up her own mind.

It was a week before the men came. From the parlour Agnes charted their progress down the street. There were four of them, working in pairs. They went in and out of the houses, sometimes disappearing for a long time, sometimes re-appearing almost immediately, and sometimes forced to remain, pinned on a doorstep, Mormon-like, uncomfortable.

When it came to her turn, Agnes saw them relax visibly as she invited them in. She smiled and they smiled back, gaining confidence. Her response when it came, was short and to the point. It caught them off guard, she saw them exchange glances, and then one said smoothly "We appreciate your frankness Mrs Watson, but please do think over what we've said. You don't need to make a decision just yet." They rose as if to a pre-arranged signal and the door closed behind them with a satisfying click.

For days there was talk of nothing else. It wasn't only Mount Street. It seemed they were all to go, the whole tight network of streets that had been Agnes' world. For she had only moved around the corner to marry Tom. She had come in a lively procession, her few belongings piled on a hand-cart and added to along the way by well-wishing neighbours. She had been proud to set up house, to have her own cool, dim parlour with the glass-bead curtain and the wine-coloured chenille table-cover.

Proud too of her tall, young husband, and later, of his smart new uniform. She had crushed into the crowd around the City Hall, waving and cheering. He would be home for Christmas. But that had been 1916, and he went to the Battle of the Somme.

Now, sixty years on, Agnes had her own battle to fight in this new war. The men from the council were patient and persevering. They worked up and down the grid of streets, nibbling away at the resistance. Each deserted house, the windows blank like empty eye-sockets, was a small triumph for reason and good sense.

Some folk went quickly - to flats or maisonettes. Others waited in a queue for new, bright, terraced houses, with shining kitchens and bathrooms and neat, pocket-handkerchief gardens. Except for Agnes. She wanted neither. The eleventh-night bonfire was the biggest ever, fed by the unending 'redding-out', but the atmosphere was strange and charged. It was an annual triumph, a grand finale and a wake, all rolled into one. Watching the flames leap high into the night sky, Agnes supposed she would have to choose in the end.

On the thirteenth she followed the Black Men at Bangor, neat and trim in her smart blue suit and her small white straw with the red and blue ribbon. The idea was at first vague and formless. But somewhere between The Esplanade and the Castle it began to crystallise and take shape. The bands played, the men marched, their fringed banners filling in the wind like square-rigged sails, and Agnes was carried along, arms and legs moving automatically to the rhythm of those around her, her mind elsewhere.

The sound of the gulls. The year she didn't march. The year she stole away to walk along the deserted beach and wander across the point.

Ballyholme - the smell of seaweed. The slow shush of the breaking waves and the rattle of pebbles moving in the backwash. The pattern of ripples and soft, spiralled, worm-casts. The damp sand that oozed and squelched between her toes.

Ballymacormick - scent of gorse and bracken. Crickets that whirred in the long grasses. A light breeze that played across her head and shoulders. Cow-parsley and cuckoo-spit and tangles of bramble bushes, the fruits still green and hard.

Groomsport - a picture-postcard arc of sand between twin points. The village clustered in the curve of the bay. Headlands dotted with caravans looking outwards, across the sea to Scotland and beyond.

A secret gallery of pictures, hanging in her mind, private and precious... Yes, Agnes decided, it was a good idea.

She read and re-read the council's explanatory notes until she was absolutely sure. The form was long and complicated. Agnes took her time, checking every detail. How much? That was the question. She had no idea.

The young man who came to discuss the compensation was hesitant and concerned. "You do understand," he began, "that compensation can only be paid to householders still here when the demolition notices are served." His tone was apologetic. "It could be quite a long time I'm afraid... months probably... It might be very difficult for you… no-one else…" He spoke carefully, choosing his words. "You might find it lonely… dangerous. Are you sure…" He stopped, not wanting to say 'you know what you're doing'. Poor old soul, he thought, it must be hard to have to move at her age.

"I want to move." She broke in as if divining his thoughts. "Only, you see, I need the money." She made tea then and talked. Listening to her, Mount Street and all its inhabitants, past and present, came alive. She entertained him, her stories witty, perceptive, sharp. And finally he named the maximum possible compensation, mentally crossing his fingers that his superior wouldn't check. Anyway, he thought, defensively, the place is shining, like a new pin. And then, curious, I wonder what she needs it for? Agnes rolled the figure around in her mind, savouring it. It was enough.

Summer slipped into autumn, autumn to winter. Agnes mapped out the days and weeks like a battle plan. The council had been defeated, but she had other, more difficult enemies. Outwardly she fought a grim war of attrition against the encroaching dust and grime, the grafitti, the ugliness, the decay. Inwardly she battled against the loneliness, the sense of isolation, the silence that spread through the streets like a slow poison and threatened to engulf her.

She set targets, achieved small victories, established new routines. She still washed on Mondays, ironed on Tuesdays, rested on Sundays. And daily she ran up her flags of defiance - the eiderdown hung out to air from the upper window. The smell of freshly-baked bread. The scrubbed strip of pavement in front of the house with its alternate red, white and blue kerbstones bright and clean. But other things changed.

One by one the signs of civilization began to dissolve. Street-lamps failed and left new pools of shadow. Drains clogged and spewed foul-smelling black ooze after heavy rain. Pigeons colonized the empty houses, gutters filled and overflowed, and green algae flourished on damp gables. And when the bin-lorry did not come to collect her rubbish, Agnes felt, finally, forgotten and alone.

She moved into the parlour, a rational response to an irrational fear that the demolition men might begin when she wasn't looking. On Sundays she went to church and prayed fervently to combat her other fear - that death might yet cheat her. With the coming of warmer weather she eked out her coal, so that only a thin wisp of smoke curled from her chimney. She laid out boundaries, invisible lines that marked the territory she could preserve from the creeping dereliction. And as her territory shrank, so her idea grew and developed. She made lists; things to find out, things to do, things to arrange. She dreamt of the convenience of a car.

When they gave Robert Keady the message that Agnes wanted to see him he felt a sudden sadness. He really had wanted her to win. Over the months his interest in the case had grown into something personal. He had even tried to explain it to Helen. She had been sympathetic and understanding. He had done all he could to speed up the process and it seemed it hadn't been enough.

Robert parked the car on the Woodstock Road and walked slowly through the deserted streets. His footsteps echoed on the empty pavements and his toes scuffed up dust. Here in the grim reality of what had become of Mount Street, her failure was not hard to understand. But rounding the corner, he stared at the house, completely taken aback. The windows sparkled, the knocker shone. These were not the gestures of defeat. He was absurdly pleased.

Agnes led him into the parlour. "I'll just wet the tea. Will you take a bit of soda?" The soda-bread was warm and oozing with butter. It dribbled through his fingers and dripped onto the plate. It tasted good. As he ate, Agnes once again talked, her words tumbling over each other. He was first startled, then amused, then, gradually, infected by her enthusiasm. He began to see that it would be possible. And yes, he would help.

*   *   *

Robert brought the demolition notice himself. He held it out to Agnes and she stood very still, biting fiercely on her lip. Now, at this last moment she began to cry, the tears welling up behind her eyes and spilling silently down her cheeks. Tears of release… excitement… joy.

*   *   *

The evening was warm and still. Agnes sat, her hands resting idly in her lap and looked out over the bay. Behind her in the doorway the glass-bead curtain hung motionless - music stilled. She had found it surprisingly easy to adapt to this new way of life. To the fire that lit at the press of a switch - living flames that flickered around perpetual coals. To hot water at the turn of a tap. To the table that folded down to become an extra bed. The tiny, apple-green toilet and shower cubicle. To Agnes it was both luxury and leisure, and she still could not decide which she appreciated most.

Her caravan, perched on the tip of the headland, was the last in a row of statics, its neat garden marked out by a low, picket fence. Agnes loved her garden - the path, edged with shells, which curved from the opening in the fence to the caravan steps, the tiny lawn, dotted with daisies, the scarlet petunias in the earthenware tubs.

Below her she saw a group of mackerel fishermen picking their way carefully over the slippery rocks. From the beach she heard the sound of children: laughter, shouting, a sudden wail. Overhead, the gulls called. Agnes watched as the sun's reflection dipped and slid under the surface of the sea. In the sudden coolness she thought of Robert and Helen. It was good to have something to leave and someone to leave it to. Someday she would answer the call of the gulls and slip quietly away with the sunset.

But not quite yet.

On Pharmacy Road

Ayisha lies on the flat roof of her grandmother's house. Despite the early hour, heat from the clay tiles burns through her thin tunic and trousers, setting her skin on fire. Each indrawn breath is a blend of heat and grit, stinging her nose, drying her throat. The dog is flopped beside her, panting, and she touches her nose to his, the cool, dampness of it welcome. His tail thumps, once, twice, raising puffs of dust so that they sneeze in unison. He is almost better now, his half-hoppity walk the only reminder of the night she found him, cowering behind the shield of empty kerosene drums, one paw trailing, the gash on his leg oozing blood.

The night her mother and would-have-been baby sister died.

She doesn't know where the dog came from - perhaps he too had been lifted by the blast from the stray shell; the blast that cast her mother under the collapsing wall at the corner of the alleyway that ran behind their house, so that she was carried home, limp and bloody, her clothes in shreds. Her legacy to Ayisha a new memory: of a dust-covered hand dangling by her side, a last look of terror in her eyes.

The dog Ayisha could save, tangling her hands in his matted fur, his whimpers stilled as she buried her head in his side, closing her eyes and ears to the sweat that blurred her mother's face, to the bundle of bloodied rags, to her grandmother's keening. For a month now he has shadowed her, waking and sleeping, his ribs receding, his rough lick a comfort; while her grandmother looks on, strangely without complaint.

Ayisha traces her name in the dust of the parapet and pokes at a beetle which lies prone, as if it too is sapped by the heat that rises in waves. Below, imprisoned within the compound wall, chickens scratch among the dusty shrubs. Beyond, Wishtan spreads: a jumble of mud-brick houses hidden among twisting alleys, their high walls guarding against the sun. A string of children, bright, like coloured beads, thread their way to the mullah's house which squats beside the one-room mosque. Yesterday she too passed through that iron gate, sat in the courtyard that serves as a school: chanted her numbers, formed her letters, listened to the reading of the Koran. Yesterday she was nine and therefore permitted to learn. Today is her tenth birthday. Today, by Taliban decree, she can no longer go to school.

She doesn't want to watch but can't help herself. At the end of the line Ahmed hangs back, turns, his hand raised, shading his eyes. Ayisha stands up: a flash of emerald against the sky; raises her hand in return, bridges the distance between them. She dips her head, a reed bending before the wind, unbroken; mouths, "Go on." He is ten today also, but a boy. She knows he's too far away to see her lips move, but her thought flies to him, his response equally swift: 'Later we will have our own school.' Another boy appears in the gateway, grabbing Ahmed's arm, and with a last backward glance, he disappears beyond the gate. Dropping to her knees she squeezes the dog more tightly, wedging Ahmed's promise between them: warm, secure.

Later, when all of Wishtan closes its shutters against the ferocity of the sun, they will huddle together in the corner of the deserted house that has become their secret place, the hoarded stump of candle guttering in the draught from the gap between the planks that board the windows, while Ahmed shares with her all he has learnt. Today and every day - at least while the summer lasts. She thrusts away the thought of winter, vows to find a way. It is a vow she cannot qualify with the usual In sha'Allah, for it seems Allah doesn't will it. Nor would their father if he was to find out.

Their father she fears more, for Allah she can't see, and so isn't sure about, although that is a sin she knows she must hide deep within her; along with her curiosity about that other, more musical God, who once danced in the sounds that drifted from the military base at the end of their road. The road the infidels call 'Pharmacy'. She remembers the silent fall of snowflakes, the jingle of bells, the lilting tunes which caused her feet to tap, and the words that, though unknown, repeated themselves in her head and made her smile.

Those soldiers are long gone, but others, they say, are coming. This time they will not roll in column down the road which, gouged through the centre of Wishtan, cuts her family in half. Few pass there now and the metal shutters that punctuate its walls rarely open. Piles of stones, three or four high, dot its length, warning of danger. She can signal from her grandmother's house to her cousins living on the other side, but can't cross to play without someone to take her.

She looks at the roofs opposite, sighs: from today, play too may be denied her.

Behind her a bang, followed by a low rumble, a grey dust cloud filling the sky. Instinctively she crouches, shushing the dog. A second rumble, a second fountain of dust: clearing, settling. She raises her head, turns towards the sound, sees a tumble of bricks scattered about a newly opened space where before there had been a clutter of roofs. A moment's silence, then running footsteps, raised voices carrying clearly in the still air. Two soldiers wave towards a gash in the wall, shout at a third. Ayisha senses shock in their voices, tinged with fear. An old woman emerges from the gap, shaking, her shayla across her face. An older man follows, his beard white-streaked, his skin creased, like paper folded many times. He stoops to tug a prayer mat from the rubble, shaking it clean.

Ayisha knows them, has played with their grandchildren, been shouted at for chasing their chickens: has wished them ill. She focuses on the prayer mat, its colours muted by the dust, thinks - is this my doing?

The old man reaches the soldiers, gestures towards the rubble. His voice is staccato-sharp, like gunfire. 'These are our homes. That one my house. My children, my grandchildren, where are they to live now?' He pauses, gathers breath.

One of the soldiers spreads his hands as if in mute apology, while another says in precise Dari, "The houses… we thought they were empty." He is scribbling on a piece of card, holds it out, "At Jackson base, you will receive compensation. We didn't know…"

The old man spits at the soldier's feet. "You know nothing."

There is a stir below, her grandmother calling, "Ayisha." She hugs the dog again, stands up slowly. Today she has new work to do. Today she must start to practise to be a woman. It is too soon, unwelcome, but she has no choice.

*   *   *

Darkness settles on Wishtan, a cloak of cold imposing its own curfew. Breaking it, two men slip silently into the kitchen of her grandparents' house. Ayisha is startled awake by voices raised in argument. One word repeated, louder than the rest, punctuated by the emphatic thump she recognizes as that of the butt of a Kalashnikov on the dirt floor: "Panjwai…" There have been other nights, other visitors: their voices low murmurs that lulled her to sleep. But tonight she shivers and crawls onto the pallet beside Ahmed, curling into him, reassured by his even breathing, by the sharp jab of his elbow in her side. Tobacco smoke eddies under her bedroom door, warning footsteps that signal her father sending her scurrying back to her own mat. She injects a faint catch into each breath, readying herself to feign an awakening at his touch. Heavy breathing above her and then a draught brushing her face, the faint click of the latch. Cautiously she opens one eye, lets out a whoosh of relief. To have been found on Ahmed's mat... her father isn't slow to wield his stick.

In the morning she slips out onto the roof again, tracks her twin's course to school, adds her address to her name drawn in the dust of the parapet. '...Sangin, Helmand.' A voice, crackling and disembodied, breaks the silence. "People of Sangin. Peace and the blessings of God be with you."

She peers over the parapet.

"...Help your Afghan brothers... bring us the hidden weapons and bombs so we can destroy them. If you do this we can help you. If not..." A high-pitched whine blanks out the voice, fades again, "...it is your choice."

She thinks of her mother, and of how she had no choice. The dog stiffens under her arm and she looks up to see Nouri looming over her, blocking out the sun.

"Your uncle is here and wishes to speak to you."

Ayisha jumps up smiling, the dog leaping beside her.

Her uncle isn't smiling. He glances towards the black-turbaned stranger watching at the window grill, and coughs, as if his mouth is dust-clogged. "We have a task for you."

She darts a look at her grandmother pummelling dough, at her grandfather running worry beads through his fingers, but neither raise their head.

"Come." Her uncle hefts a bulging sack and slams the door behind them, sticking out his foot to stop the dog from escaping, the puzzled yelps trailing them along the alley. His grip on her arm is tight, as if he does not trust her to follow, and when she looks up at him he looks away, so that her question dies in her throat. In the deserted alley, the windows of the houses planked, he stops, nods towards a door that sags on its hinges. "You know this place?"

She looks down at the scuffed markings in the dust, a perfect match for her sandals, recognizes the impossibility of denial. He doesn't wait for her answer, but is already edging open the door, gesturing the stranger in, indicating the boarded window, the narrow gap between the bottom two planks.

The stranger nods. "It's ok." He bends down to the base of the wall, pokes at the mud with his penknife, forms an almost invisible hole. He nods again, disappears outside and Ayisha hears him scrabbling in the dirt. The question forms in her head: what do they want from me? Understanding washing cold over her as thin wires poke through the hole, waving like scorpion antennas.

"You can do this, Ayisha?" Her uncle is lifting a makeshift plunger from the sack, attaching the wires. He rests his hands on her shoulders, stares into her eyes. "You know how it is. Last week, Panjwai. Yesterday, the houses destroyed. Tomorrow…" he shakes his head, "We will show them we do not abandon our brothers." He pushes her down to crouch on the floor, her eyes level with the peephole gap. "Soldiers will come - in one hour, maybe two. When the first one reaches the corner…" he punches downwards. "You understand? If it was not school day, we would entrust this to Ahmed." His voice hardens, "As it is… you are honoured."

*   *   *

85

It is a long time to wait, a long time to think. She kneels by the window, her eye pressed against the slit, focusing on the strip of wall that is her marker, her finger hovering over the plunger. She remembers yesterday: the old woman, the single tear that tunnelled through the dust on her cheeks. Remembers also the fading newspaper pictures of Panjwai tacked to the schoolroom wall: the first, of a bare room, a lone figure hunched over a charred circle on the floor; the next, a child's foot protruding from a blanket in the back of an open truck, and in the last, an impotent crowd filling a narrow street, silent, though screaming. She nurses the mother and baby-shaped hole in her heart, says, "I can do this."

*   *   *

Her knees are aching, her back stiff, but she doesn't move for fear she will miss her moment. Off to her left the unmistakeable scrape of a ladder against a wall, the metallic creaking as someone climbs. There is a shouted question, a pause, an indistinct reply, then the soft thud as the climber returns to ground level. She knows now where they are, that it is a matter of minutes only. The first soldier appears, his clothing and skin sand-coloured, his face beardless. - Because he is a foreigner? Or because he is too young? She cannot tell. He steps slowly, deliberately, as the old do, swinging a metal circle attached to a long pole from side to side in front of him; each following soldier stepping carefully in his tracks. They have the look of youth, of her cousin Sahid. She fixes her eyes on the bend in the road, rests the palm of her hand on the plunger, tries to make her mind blank.

The line falters, the soldier nearest Ayisha hunkering down, hand outstretched. The following soldier calls out and she doesn't need to understand the words to sense his fear. She squints through the gap, sees a dog nosing along the opposite wall. Catches her breath. But this dog has four good legs, walks straight. The hunkering soldier steps out of line, strokes the dog's head, slides one arm under the belly and scoops him into his arms. He stands up, his breathing shallow, and adjusting the dog to a more secure position, inches forwards. The dog barks once, settles in the soldier's arms and she hesitates, her eyes darting along the line, allowing the first soldier to pass beyond her line of vision. The second also, and the third, her uncle's voice hammering in her head, "Panjwai... we do not abandon... you are honoured." The one cradling the dog is half-way to safety, and still she waits, until he too has disappeared. There are only three soldiers left. She sees the face of the turbaned stranger who accompanied her uncle, his mouth a

87

snarl, and belatedly presses the plunger, shutting her eyes against the succession of flashes, the choking clouds of dust. Small flames, like spent fireworks, flicker in the line of blackened holes threading the road. One soldier is being supported towards the corner, dragging his leg. The final one staggers behind, clutching his ears. From beyond the corner Ayisha hears a soft 'shush, shush', the dog's high-pitched yowl fading to a whimper. She imagines him wriggling up the soldier's chest, their faces touching, a pink tongue licking thanks. She disconnects the plunger, and careful to follow her final instructions, stuffs it into the sack, coiling the ends of wire and burying them in the dust floor.

As the heat bleeds out of the sun, silence settling over Wishtan, she slips home rehearsing her report: exaggerating injuries, practising an apologetic shrug.

Celebrity Status.

9.56 am.

They're waiting for me at the gate. The solicitor says I'm off my head, agreeing to talk to reporters, but I *have* to - for Brenda as well as me. They'll crucify me anyway, whether I talk to them or not, but this way, at least I'll have had my say.

I just need a minute to set things straight in my mind - from the beginning.

*   *   *

It was a headline in the paper - 'Tyrone goes wild!' I had to laugh. Here was me just spent, reluctantly I might add, £5.00 on a licence for my wife's poodle - a mincing, yappy little beast - and this John-James O'Bryne can keep a *lion* for free. Now that *is* bureaucracy gone mad. But then what can you expect from yon boys in the civil service - I've always said if they'd a brain between them they'd be dangerous.

I wouldn't have thought any more about it, if it hadn't been for the wee ad in the Penny a Word's. It's become a bit of a habit, reading them after the sports pages: following the trail of the 'Royal Albert Country Rose' tea-sets - 'unwanted gifts' - which seem to circulate around the province. I'd never had the nerve to get rid of ours. I might have missed it but for next door's cat appearing at our window, miaowing and posturing; so that Mitzi, who had been stretched out on the hearth-rug, leapt up to attack the glass, and managed to knock my mug of tea over, highlighting the ad. - 'Tiger cubs, male/female, £200 / £250' and a box number. I remember thinking: Now *that* would put her nose out of joint.

I wrote the letter at work, imagining Brenda's reaction - Henry Johnson... Mr Ordinary himself... A tiger tamer?... Catch a grip."

But I was tired of being ordinary, and what was good enough for Omagh was good enough for East Belfast... I could see myself now... the talk of the town... a celebrity.

The reply took six days - I could've walked there and back quicker; but I was lucky; it came on a Saturday, so I got to it before Brenda saw there was something other than bills. I began to have visions of myself as a latter-day George

Adamson, but I couldn't quite see Brenda as Virginia McKenna - pity. Anyway, the first thing was to get to Castledearg.

A wee fly run in a works van and I found the place no bother. The size of six weeks cubs was a bit of a shock, though *nothing* to the size of the mother so I realised I'd have to re-think the garden-shed sized cage I'd planned. Not a problem, for we never used the back yard anyway. Evening sunshine, in the height of summer, warmed an area of flags big enough to take a table and a couple of chairs, but the flex of the tele isn't long enough, and it's been a good few years since Brenda would miss 'Emmerdale' to sit in the yard with me. I kept a few tools in the old outside toilet but I could soon sort that out. I reckoned that if I worked every evening it would take me a fortnight to get the cage ready, which was fine as they wouldn't let me take the cub till the cheque cleared anyway. We set a date and I went home well satisfied.

I'd like to have seen Brenda's face when B+Q delivered the timber and the narrow-gauge wire mesh. It was still pretty impressive when I came home. She stood on the back doorstep, her folded arms resting on her chest, her feet planted, widespread, on the mat.

"What are you playing at?"

I didn't mind being shouted at for *something*. "Wait and see" I said, "Its a surprise." It would be a surprise - definitely one up to me.

Every evening that week and the next I was out in the yard, working away. When Brenda was in the kitchen I beat out rhythms with my hammer and whistled extra loudly, interspersing 'Danny Boy' and 'A Long Way to Tipperary' with rousing hymn tunes, as if I was practising for the Twelfth.

I enjoyed myself.

And in a funny sort of a way I think Brenda did too. It was like a game: at first she pretended she wasn't interested, then she tried to trick me into letting the secret out; but for once I was man enough for her. That was a new experience for both of us and I spun it out as long as I could. She could tell it had to be a pet - any fool could have worked that one out, but as to what kind - she hadn't a clue. The day I dragged home the fallen limb, scrunched up dead leaves still clinging stubbornly to the spreading fan of spindly branches, I overheard her telling Annie next door,

"I think he's building an aviary... for my birthday."

I hadn't remembered her birthday, but it wasn't such a bad idea, so to keep her going I didn't trim off all the smaller branches before cementing the large limb into the centre of the yard. While I put the finishing touches to the enclosure, Brenda sat at the back door, her foot tracing the cobweb-thin shadow-branches which drifted on the polished flags.

On the Saturday morning, I said, "I've a message to do in Castledearg, I'll not be back till near tea-time. How about a special meal... a bit of a celebration?"

She beamed and didn't even ask how I was getting there, and I got out quick, before I changed my mind. Brenda has a lovely smile, but I couldn't tell you how long it had been since she'd turned it on me.

It rained all the way to Castledearg. The windscreen wipers on the van jerked and scraped across the glass and I imagined the scratching noise might be something like the sound of the tiger sharpening her claws on the limb I'd brought for her - it made it bearable. On the way home the tiger cub dozed in the back like an over-sized, contented tabby - they'd given her a wee dose to keep her quiet. At the supermarket I stocked up with two cases of Whiskas and twelve packets of powdered milk. That should keep us going for a week or two. I was almost home when I remembered a card. The wee corner shop isn't exactly 'Clintons' but the bright, splashy parrot, with "Happy Birthday To You" in a large speech bubble was perfect. I decided to go in through the back and put the tiger in the cage 'till we'd had our meal and then go round and in the front again. No point in spoiling a good dinner by surprising Brenda too soon.

Afterwards, as we went out into the yard, I made Brenda shut her eyes. The tiger was barely awake and staggered drunkenly towards us, her short legs buckling. I commanded Brenda, "Hold out your hands."

As I placed the tiger cub in her arms her eyes flew open. She was speechless... It was wonderful. She stared down into the gold-flecked eyes staring unblinkingly back at her, and then she looked at me and smiled. Actually smiled. I was the one speechless then. It was the last thing I would have expected.

"You've bought a tiger... for me."

She was stroking its head, the downy fur flattening and springing again under her hand. When it began to purr, I realised that somehow, unbelievably, when I least intended to, I'd done something *right*. What had begun as a middle-aged act of defiance had turned me into some sort of a hero. Mitzi began to be neglected as the tiger did for us what the baby would've done years before.

Every evening we were in the yard, like proud parents, feeding, cleaning, playing with Ginny; enjoying our new-found status and, increasingly, each other. The distance between us began to rewind like retractable cord, gaining momentum steadily until the evening I brought home the delayed action photograph - Brenda on the lounger, looking down at Ginny cradled in her arms, me hunkered beside her, watching them both, one arm lying lightly along her shoulder. Brenda's face crumpled and I moved to hold her as, for the first and last time, she cried - a healing well of tears that filled up the baby-shaped chasm that lay between us, and washed it away.

And all through the long spring and early summer Ginny grew and grew. We were proud of her condition, even if feeding her was costing us a small fortune. Her fur was sleek and shining, her eyes bright. When we went into the cage she would drop from her perch, the branches ricocheting upwards behind her, and roll onto her back purring, so that Brenda could run her fingers through her soft stomach hair. Sometimes she would spring away again and lie for a moment along a branch, teasing, just out of reach, her tail drawing a swinging arch across the flags. But as she matured we had to be more careful. Her claws were long and sharp and she would sometimes scratch without meaning to. Once or twice she whimpered as we went back inside, prowling up and down the yard, growling softly.

One Sunday we went for a walk on the embankment. Ginny shied in and out of the long shadows and twined herself and her lead round and round our legs. But so many people stared that Brenda was frightened someone would report us to the council - our lease said 'No Pets'. We didn't take her out again.

As Ginny developed, so did we. My work, once an escape, became a necessary distraction from our evenings with Ginny and the nights by ourselves: rediscovering old pleasures, awakening fresh desires. Afterwards, as we lay, her face on my chest, my head tucked into her shoulder, we would talk and laugh and plan, before slipping into sleep. I wished we could take Ginny out again, but Brenda was adamant. And hero or no hero I didn't argue. Neither of us wanted to lose her.

*   *   *

It was a Thursday. The ice-cream van was playing as I arrived home from work. Children pushed and jostled to get to the head of the queue while I stood at the back, humming to myself in time, with the distant bands marching on the Ormeau

Road - preliminary skirmishes before the Twelfth. Tapping my foot to the pulse of the Lambeg drums, I imagined leading Ginny at the head of the procession, with a gold rope and a purple-studded collar, as if we'd stepped straight out of a banner. Maybe next year, if she could be trained.

The ice-cream was beginning to drip as I went into the kitchen. Licking both cones, I walked through to the yard.

And stopped.

Brenda lay, crumpled against the frame of the cage. From under her head a dark stain spread out over the slabs like a gigantic ink-blot. Ginny lay beside her, one paw placed protectively on Brenda's chest. She was licking Brenda's face and I could see traces of where blood had run in rivulets from four jagged tears in her scalp. Sunlight, spilling over the back wall, illuminated them like a scene from a medieval morality play. Brenda's normally mousy hair shone, and the dark congealed stripes mirrored the pattern of the sleek head beside her. The split shadow of the overhanging branch vee'd out on either side of them, the jagged gap in the middle raw and fresh. I don't know how long I stood, not moving; absorbing Brenda's immobility, the alabaster pallor of her skin, the horrible finality evident in the curled fingers stiffly clawing the wire mesh;

while the ice-cream melted and ran down my arm and dripped unnoticed onto my trousers. I think I must have screamed, for Ginny lifted her head and I saw the fur rise in a straight line down the ridge of her back. She shifted her paw in an unmistakeable gesture of possession and I dropped the cones and fled.

*   *   *

I'm the talk of the town all right. A real celebrity. The police can't decide whether there's anything they can charge me with, but the Executive's working on a bill to make the 'Dangerous Animals Act' apply to Northern Ireland before there's another tragedy.

And the reporters at the gate? They want my side of the story, or so they say. As for what I can tell them - I don't believe Ginny meant to hurt Brenda... I can't believe that... But the house is very quiet - too quiet.

Mitzi sits in the yard where Brenda and Ginny died and refuses to budge. She doesn't yap any more; I wish she did.

Aftermath

She went up the stairs quietly, wearily, automatically missing the creaking third step, pulling on the handrail to cover the extra stretch. She seldom forgot now, unlike the early days, his voice reminding her, chiding and complaining of being woken. It hadn't mattered that it wasn't true, she still felt guilty.

In the early days she'd felt so much guilt but now she could move about the house ghost-like, with scarcely a sound, dusting and cleaning, while in the quietness he drowsed, days and nights almost indistinguishable, his senses dulled, his pain eased. She could be glad of that.

At the top of the stairs she paused. It was part of her daily ritual, this stopping to decide whether to turn right or left. It all came to the same thing in the end, but in the months when so little she did was by choice it had become important to her. Left then, to Johnnie's room first - unnaturally tidy for a nine-year old, but he was a quiet child and tried in his own way to lessen her burden.

In the dim light filtering through the pulled-down blind she couldn't help smiling at his clumsy attempt to straighten his quilt. The cover was pulled neatly over the bed, the downie underneath a series of bumps and bulges in the middle. It was always the same: morning by morning she removed the cover, shook out the downie and tucked it in again against the wall, taking care as she moved the bed to lift it so as not to make a scraping sound on the floor. Night by night he turned the quilt into a landscape of hills and valleys, squashed and bulged and twisted at random. Sometimes, when she stopped to think about it, it worried her. But today the familiar sight was oddly reassuring.

Mechanically she moved from room to room, straightening, tidying, folding. It was all just as it had been for months - Catherine's discarded clothes, Michael's half-built models which she had to be careful to step over and, in their own room, the desk with its clutter of books and papers. Just as it had been, except for the strange, grey half-light and, when she opened his door, the absolute silence.

She hesitated on the threshold, then entered with a slight, involuntary squaring of her shoulders. It looked and felt the same: the array of bottles on the dressing table, the commode in the corner, the makeshift buzzer by the bedside lamp. All the paraphernalia of the sick room and the faint sweet smell she had neither been able to trace, nor to eradicate. It was all the same, all except the empty bed, the covers thrown back.

She shivered. Standing there she had a vision of the wasted body, the face shrunken and hollow, skin parchment-yellow, veins prominent. She heard the voice, thin and querulous, a man made small and old before his time. She shook her head to dispel the image and forced herself to focus on the bed. It was empty, empty, empty… She repeated the word like a litany, to convince herself it was over, finally over.

She began to work her way around the room methodically - sink, bedside table, commode. She would have liked to remove the commode but it was awkward and heavy and in any case she didn't know what to do with it. But the bottles she could deal with, emptying and discarding, the various liquids a technicolour stream in the sink. Then she attacked the bed, stripping back blankets and sheets, piling them in a heap in the middle of the floor. There had been so many layers, a futile attempt to combat the increasing coldness he felt, a coldness which came from his body and not the room. It was so much easier now that she didn't have to manoeuvre around his frailty. Even with help it had been difficult, as well as being demeaning and uncomfortable for him.

As a child she had disliked changing beds, a regular Monday morning chore that made her hate Mondays. Lately, with every day a 'Monday' these feelings had returned, stronger, harder. Once, as she went to lift the clean linen from the cupboard, she had to lock the bathroom door and tense and relax her muscles again and again to release the hard knot in her stomach and to still her rising panic. She had come to see the changing of the bed as a symbol of their imprisonment, he in the bed and she circling, unable to move beyond the reach of his summons, as the days blended into weeks and the weeks into months.

She had been out - quick forays to the supermarket, the chemist, the Gas Board, all essential journeys, all rushed. Always at the back of her mind the picture of the neighbor waiting, the pillows needing to be fluffed up, covers needing to be straightened, the draw-sheet to change. Somehow over the months the focus of the house had shifted so that the bed, his bed, had become the centre around which everything else rotated.

Today she felt a release as layer after layer of bedclothes joined the pile on the floor. She felt lighter, almost dizzy. With a half-suppressed skip around the bare mattress she gathered up the discarded linen, took it downstairs and shoved it thankfully into the washing machine. The final click of the door, the noise of the water, the slow turning of the drum was, for the first time in months, a relief, a joy.

She turned and caught a sound coming from the front of the house, the scrunch of gravel as someone came towards the front door. She stiffened and stood very still as she saw the outline of a figure through the frosted glass. She saw it bend, distort, then straighten as a pile of envelopes dropped through the letter-box onto the square of light inside the door. She began to move up the hall towards them then froze as she saw the silhouette of an arm raised to the knocker and heard the light rat-tat-tat.

Sometimes the postman had been the only person she'd spoken to all day. His cheery, 'Morning', 'Cold out', or 'Just bills I'm afraid', her only fragile contact with the outside world. Today she would see more than sympathy in his friendly gaze, have to respond to his likely awkward condolences, and all the usual formulae of bereavement. She couldn't face that yet. So she remained where she was, holding her breath until he turned away and the sound of his retreating footsteps faded.

Gathering up the mail she carried it into the sitting room. It was cold, dull, cheerless. Around the edges of the blinds fine lines of sunlight slanted across the floor, needle-thin, serving only to emphasise the gloom. The ashes of Tuesday's fire lay in the grate, the charred remains of a log in one corner, grey-white dust spilling through the bars onto the tiles. She glanced around the room and then down at the mail in her hands. As she slit the envelopes, the pictures began to blur, the words merging into each other. 'So sorry to hear', 'Sad loss', 'With sympathy', 'A time to grieve'. She gave a choking noise, half-sob, half-laugh. She had had plenty of time to grieve through these last months, watching him waste and fade and change. Watching hope turn to fear, realization to anger, and finally, bitterness to apathy. Hearing his voice - once strong, cheerful, loving - become weak, pitiful, thin. Seeing him become someone she didn't know, someone she'd never known.

A long shudder ran through her. She had not lost him now, she had lost him a long time ago. And now… now it wasn't grief she felt. Laying the cards down she bent to the hearth and raked out the ashes. A fire, that was what she wanted, what she needed. There were only sticks in the kindling box. She looked around for something, anything to start the fire. The cards lay on the sideboard, conventional and predictable. On impulse she began to crumple them into the grate, criss-crossing the sticks over them. They caught on the third match and she watched in satisfaction as the sticks crackled and flared, the logs catching one by one until the fire burned steadily - warm, bright, alive.

The flames danced and spun, casting patterns of light and shade around the room. She sat down, automatically tugging at the ill-fitting cover on the chair, the ugly, oh so protective stretch cover which hid the bold Sanderson print. Before, when he was downstairs, the covers were needed, and when he stopped coming down they had remained. Leaving them on preserved the fiction of hope: removing them would have seemed a gesture of defeat. And so they had stayed - sturdy, useful, dull. It would only take a few minutes...

She began to tug at the knots on the ties at the back of the first cushion. They had tightened with time and seemed perversely to tighten further as she tried to work them loose - first with her nails, then with her teeth. Finally, exasperated, she reached for the scissors from the sideboard drawer. Down the tunnel of years she heard her mother's voice - firm, practical, frugal. 'Knots shouldn't need to be cut, all that is required is time and a little patience.' She saw the deft fingers as they teased and worked at tangled threads and the flush of satisfaction as they were released, the smug tone, 'There, I told you. Just time and a little patience.'

She wondered, briefly, how much time and patience her mother would have had in these last months and if it would have stretched to this. Well, hers did not. It felt almost like vandalism to cut the ties, but vandalism she discovered with a sudden gleam of humour, could be satisfying too. She hadn't remembered how vivid the print was. The bold peacock tails were fanned out on each cushion, the colours strong against the background and where the pencil-line of light slipping around the edge of the blind caught the piping it glowed, like a fine gold frame. She glanced towards the window. The suite had always looked best in sunlight. She remembered the day they chose it, he and she standing together under the large store windows, the light emphasising and enhancing the colours.

"It's my treat," he'd said. "To thank you both for taking me in."

And she had laughed and squeezed his arm and replied, "It's no trouble dad," and tried to forget the momentary, sad smile she had glimpsed on his face. By the window now, only the thought of the neighbours stopped her releasing it and letting the light flood in. Instead, to compensate, she lit the lamps and the room seemed to fill with colour and warmth, to become welcoming and familiar, her own room again.

In the kitchen the debris of a hurried breakfast still lay on the table and the faint tang of burnt toast hung in the air. The smell reminded her of something… She frowned for a moment, concentrating, and then it came to her - that hotel, two years ago. Their last weekend away and the friendly waitress who had tried to talk her into having a cooked breakfast.

"Don't eat enough to feed a sparrow, you don't, and you paying for it too."

She smiled at the memory and quite suddenly felt hungry. "Well now, Bridget, Theresa," she said into the silence. "I'll be having that breakfast today." As the bacon, sausages, mushrooms and tomatoes sizzled under the grill she cleared and re-set the table, humming softly. She laid a table mat and napkin and took the ivory-handled cutlery from the drawer. She lifted out her good china, and cut a slice of lemon for her tea. As she reached for the tea-pot stand the tall, single stem glass caught her eye. It was rarely used, but she would use it now. In the garden she picked a single ivory rose, just beginning to open and a stem of asparagus fern, spring-green and delicate. They made the perfect centre-piece.

Standing back and looking at the table only one thing was missing, Outside she could hear the starlings and the tits chittering in the sunshine. She stood very still for a moment, hesitating, and then very gently pulled on the blind. She let it go and it slid upwards, winding round and round the bar and out of reach. She sat down at the table, warm sunlight pouring over her. She felt giddy, she wanted to laugh aloud - she felt free. She felt as if by letting light into the room, she had let much more than light out of it.

Tomorrow she would weep and say and do all the 'right', the conventional things. But for today and for now she was just glad to be alive.

Finding Rose

Dust and cobwebs in an empty room. Nothing else, apart from a carriage-clock on the mantle-shelf, dredged, by the clearing of the masonry, in stour as fine as confectioner's sugar. Disappointment cut a swathe through my anticipation, which had built steadily since the reading of my mother's will, with the bequest of a house I hadn't known existed. Apparently let for many years, it stood empty and available. An unexpected opportunity neither Anthony nor I wished to let slip. The excitement of exploration had followed; yet as we moved from room to room, Anthony tapping and measuring and sketching ideas with his hands, I found my pleasure tempered by momentary, perplexing flashes, as if of recognition.

He was pragmatic, "This was your uncle's house. You've maybe been here when you were very young. Give it time, clearer memories may come."

He carpeted the library floor with drawings for extension and improvement - a new kitchen, an indoor closet, a terrace on the west side; and I continued my wanderings, searching for I knew not what. Until I made the discovery of two windows on the outside of the house that couldn't be accounted for within. Intrigued afresh, I paced out the long corridor and the rooms that led off it, and found a corresponding discrepancy: marked by a slight irregularity in the passageway wall, noticeable only as a faint shadow cast as the sun dipped low at dusk. And so to today, and the four long hours we waited, as the men removed the bricks, one by one, revealing the hidden doorway. Anthony watched with the professional interest of an architect, I with a mixture of excitement and anxiety. Now we stood in silence, the dust settling on our shoulders, and surveyed the emptiness of that lost room.

Anthony squeezed my shoulder and smiled his crooked smile. "No deep, dark secrets in your family then." He drew me towards the door, nodding to the men hovering in the passage, "Thank you. We'll leave you in peace to clear up."

I halted in the opening, unease hardening to a certainty. "There *must* be something here. Else why would it be blocked up?" A torn curl of wallpaper stirred in the draught from the newly opened casement and as it brushed against my fingers I pulled at it, as a child might, peeling it from the wall like an apple paring. Belshazzar-like we stared at the writing thus revealed, the import of the words as obscure.

...*leave... listen... stop.*

All thought of clearance forgotten we worried away at the crimped edges of the wallpaper. Writing flowed down the wall in neat copper-plate script, a procession of words in which the tails of the 'p's and the 'f's and the curling 'g's finished on an imaginary line exactly half-way between the rows.

The light is failing now, as it always does at this hour, the sun slipping behind the trees on Gogar Hill. I do not want to stop, tormented as I am by a new fear, that came upon me this morning as I listened to Henry's broken wheeze, that our time may be cut short. And though I will leave this house gladly, I will miss the voices echoing from the shadows - Henry, Mattie, and little Anne.

I stopped, the name washing over me, ice-cold. Henry I knew as the uncle whose house it had been, but 'Mattie.' Matthilde? His sister perhaps? Another child who shared my name?

Anthony shot a glance at my face, became matter of fact. "Let's see how much there is."

We stripped a small section of each wall. On all four the same precise handwriting in violet ink: phrases like pieces of glass in a kaleidoscope, waiting only to be tumbled for the pattern to appear. The words, full of cadences and movement, held a strange hypnotic appeal:

We have come to the point where China dies…
God forgive me…
They call me poor Rose…

Rose? Henry's wife. The un-talked of blemish on an otherwise blameless family. Whose mention closed conversations as abruptly as a slammed door. Questions multiplied in my mind, the phrase *'Henry, Mattie, and little Anne'* a constant, unsettling refrain. It was impossible to guess where the true beginning lay, so we stationed ourselves at opposite points of the room, like twin tips of a compass needle. Sometimes we had to pick the paper off in slivers, uncovering the text word by word, at others it came away in long swathes. It was Anthony who found a beginning of sorts:

It pours today, as it did that first day - when great drops cracked against the windows like gunshots, and the view, said to be the finest in the county, disappeared into the sky as if wiped from a canvas. Bored and disconsolate, an outing to Portobello abandoned, I welcomed with interest the jangle of the bell, and the stranger who stood silhouetted in the entrance, his hair silvered with rain.

We set to in earnest, working side-by-side, Rose's presence growing stronger with each column uncovered, the story unfolding as a many-layered thing.

What should I say of Henry? Washed up on the shore of father's generosity, the house came alive with his laughter, echoed with his tales of far-off, fabled places. I listened and longed, and yes… had the temerity to pray.

As I read aloud, she began to solidify, emerging from the shadows in a strangely familiar rustle of skirts, image piling on image. I saw her first in sprigged muslin:

I think often of the house on the moors where I grew, tall enough and straight; not head-turningly beautiful as sister-in-law Kate, nor even pretty like Ellie, so that it was with satisfaction that I heard it gossiped that the young Mr Still paid me some attention.

Then in striped poplin:

...the Rose I was then, young and wayward, riding astride on Firefly, racing across the moor, reckless and unafraid. Henry's dark eyes on mine accepting the challenge. Returning disheveled and drookit, so that father, capitulating, wished him well of me.

Those pictures I carried into my dreams along with an inexplicable sadness, that lay as a weight on my chest, so that I woke fighting for breath. It was on the third day that I uncovered a second reference to my own mother and the first conscious stirrings of fear:

Kate received us when we made the pilgrimage to Seton, Mattie but two months old. But as she sat, convalescent after her fifth 'disappointment', her beauty marred by a mouth pinched tight as if she sucked on a sour plum, I stopped feeling sorry for her and, God forgive me, despised her childless state - I reap what I have sowed.

It rained heavily again that night, and in the rain another dream, illumined in a lightning flash: a carriage wheel spinning, the spokes fracturing the image of a man folded on the ground, rain washing his face clean. Further away a whey-faced woman bent over a bundle, and further still, a doll lay, without an arm. Footsteps and voices and lights that flickered; a cluster of people around a bed; and far away and faint, the cry of a child.

I woke at first light, a sense of urgency upon me, which Anthony, regarding me with sympathy, sought to moderate. But hunger was nothing to the unease that gnawed at me, and so, breakfast ignored, we returned to the task.

It was as if Rose stood beside me as I teased at the paper, her clothing altering with the mood of the writing.

I saw her in purple silk:

The Rose I am now, soured they say, or perhaps wandered - by widowhood, by the loss of my children.

And in autumn-brown taffeta:

Mary is with me still, and Cameron and Archie, and I am grateful for it. They tell me Kate came, in the aftermath of the accident, to possess the house, forbidding any but her own servants to the rooms where we lay; yet afterward returned to Seton in some haste.

Now in winter worsted, sombre threads woven through the coarse cloth:

Of those dark days I remember little, only Mary's 'shush, shush' as a constant backdrop to my dreams, in which I screamed and thrashed and beat my head upon the floor. Kate did not trouble us again.

In lilac angora wool, prickly, defensive:

They think of me as 'poor Rose'. I see it in their eyes as I move up the south aisle of the kirk to the family pew. But I am Rose Still, wife (though but in name) of a husband who yet lives, and thus I take my place. I will not give the gossips the satisfaction of driving me into a less prominent seat. Nor will I wear the dull clothes their narrow propriety demands. Henry would not wish it. And nor do I.

At twelve Anthony insisted I eat, and in truth I was glad to stop, for my mind was packed tight with images of Rose, my ears ringing with the sound of her voice. Of uncle Henry's premature death I knew, though long ago and not talked of. It seemed he had suffered some form of paralysis:

The doctor was here again, and others with him. They poked and prodded and shook their heads and whispered behind their hands. They think I do not understand their talk, but Henry is not some piece of baggage to be lifted and laid and moved from place to place.

I shall not let them take him away. He did not ask for injury and his place is here. Though it be the end of our hopes, my place is here also. With Cameron and Mary to aid me I shall manage.

I found a reference to the clock:

The clock, chosen for its broken chime, ticks away the minutes and hours more quickly, as Henry grows ever more childlike. I am his parent now, and if I dream of Mattie and of Anne, it is my own blame.

The thought that perhaps I had been named for a dead cousin was macabre and unsettling. But worse - if I *was* Mattie, who was Anne?

There was an abrupt change of tone, as if deliberate, to a new and puzzling thread, which, though it vexed me, yet when I pictured her it was in shantung silk, shot through with colour:

I have come to the point where China dies. Tomorrow, before sunrise, we will pass through the Great Wall, leaving behind the gates of Jiayuguan, their curving roofs soaring against the sky. We will travel west into the wilderness, feared by the native bearers as the habitation of barbarians; but I have no despairing message to score into the brick, for we have long wished to follow this road. The names on our route already possess me - Hami, Turfan, Korla, Aksu, Kashgar - I yearn to see them all.

This passage, and others in like vein covered almost half a wall, so that I began to doubt her sanity, until finally:

This will be our last Christmas and I have planned that we will spend it in Vienna. There will be music and dancing and the sun sparkling on frosted snow. We shall see the Schonbrunn, walk in the Gloriette Colonnade, visit Prince Eugene's Belvedere and worship the Christ child in the Schottenkirche. It was long a desire of Henry's, so by my tongue and pen we will go there together, as we have gone on other travels: fleeing his crippled body and his captive mind.

I could not stop then, for in the fragmentary nature of the passages that followed I sensed that we approached the truth at last. I imagined Rose, her dress the colour of clotted blood, her hand up-stretched against the wall, her sleeve fallen back from her thinning wrist, the thread of thought broken as she paused to flex her fingers or stooped to re-fill her pen:

They say he does not hear. Yet I like to think that I have seen his eyelids flicker when I tell him that Mattie is

118

grown strong again, that Anne toddles behind her in the garden and talks the greatest of nonsense in the most serious of tones. I tell him that I no longer need a cane on any but the roughest of ground. And that at least is true. I ask forgiveness, and his blessing to send me on my way.

Memory is the cruelest thing. Of all our days that one is the clearest: the promise of sunshine breaking through the clouds. Mattie clambering onto the seat cushions, her doll clutched tight. Two-month Anne lying across my lap, blue eyes wide, her thumb firmly in her mouth.

The Grey Mare's Tale thundering down the mountainside, spray hanging in the air like dew. The sky turned ominous and the inn with the room that smelt of mice and mildew, where I would not let my children sleep, not even for one night. Henry, against his better judgement, bowing to my pleas. The horses, dipping their heads against the driving rain. The roar of water and the rush of tumbling stones; the road become a river-bed. The jarring and jolting and a horse's high-pitched scream. The blackness that swallowed me for a time, before vomiting me upon my bed, so that I thought at first I dreamt.

It was Anthony who uncovered the phrase that indicated my place in it all. He wrapped his arms around me and held me against his chest as I read:

The grave is not a dream. Mary stands at my shoulder, her grip tight and I feel the shudder of her tears. It is a pitiful thing: a mound of earth covered with clods, a clump of daffodils dying slowly in a pewter jug. The stone they say must wait for the ground to settle. It hurts me to think of it, the weight of earth pressing down on them, and I cry for Mattie, for she is afraid of the dark. God knows I did not mean to put them there. They share a coffin as they shared a cot. God keep them both.

I had always been afraid of the dark, a fear my mother termed irrational and not deserving of sympathy. Unable to wait, even for a moment, we went out to search the overgrown plot hard by the boundary of our policies, where a cluster of family graves sagged against the wall. The one we sought was tucked into the corner, smaller than the rest and half-smothered in ivy. I knelt and tugged at the suckers clinging to the surface of the stone, heedless of the fragments falling around me, praying that there might be some mistake.

'Matthilde, born March 18th 1851
Anne born February 22nd 1853
beloved daughters of Henry and Rose Still.
Cruelly taken April 20th 1853.
Together in death.'

"Cruelly taken, indeed." Anthony's grip on my hand was tight, his voice grim.

I cannot describe how it was to stand by my own grave and to feel the foundations of my life crumble. Only that I fled: from my memory of Kate, beautiful indeed, but rotten, it seemed, at the core; and from the image of Rose, dressed in black satin, her skin transparent as skimmed milk, the sound of her crying mingling with my own.

Anthony found me, his touch on my arm gentle, but firm, as he drew me back to finish the task. He stood by my side as I uncovered the final paragraphs, the words blurring:

Henry has travelled beyond me now and soon the vultures will come to strip the house bare. There is talk of providing something more suited to my needs. Though Cameron has papered over all that I have written, I have extracted a promise from him that he will build up the door. This tale is not for them. They may do as they please with the house and with the inheritance, for I shall not be here. Only Cameron and Mary know of my plan.

Ours is a hard religion. No priest to stand between, no pardon to be bought. I must make my own peace. With Henry; with the children; and with God. Word came today: I am among those chosen to accompany Florence Nightingale to Scutari. We sail on October 21st. What little skills I have learned these past months may be useful there. Though how it will weigh in the balances, I cannot tell.

The pieces of the jigsaw are falling into place, one by one. Fragments of memory coalescing into a new past, that as yet I find hard to fully embrace. Anthony talks of tracing Cameron or Mary, of travelling to Scutari; arguing that the truth will set me free. I think of Rose, in grey alpaca, tending to a soldier with one leg, the white of her apron contrasting with the brown-streaked bandages swathing his bloodied stump. And I pray that she found her peace. That I will be able to find mine.

We need to Talk

Sunetra consults the cast list lying on the table and scans the line of waiting children, looking for 'Fagin'. The boy is thin and gangly, with a narrow face, his cheekbones prominent - a good choice, at least as far as appearance goes. He sits on the chair facing her, unabashed by her stare. "Frown." She says. Obediently he screws up his face and she steps back, her head to one side, eyes half-closed, her close-cropped hair starling-sleek under the theatrical lights. She imagines the lines brown-etched, gauges the effect. The boy is altering his face in a rapid series of contortions, and she raises her hand. "Stop!"

He freezes, mid-grimace, three faces too late.

Encouraging him she says, "That was good, but too fast for me. Try again, slowly this time."

He pulls expressions, stretching them out like strands of toffee, as if enjoying the shape and feel of them.

"That's it. Now - hold." Deftly she strokes colour into the furrows on his forehead, tapering the lines outwards. She works quickly, blending pan sticks on the palm of her hand, adding, shading, smoothing; a touch here, a smudge with the edge of her finger there, a final flourish of powder which tickles his nose and makes him sneeze. "Ok, off you go." In her head she has rolled up and filed his image before he has slipped from the chair, her next character already taking shape. She enjoys working with children: the challenge of their unpredictability, the amusement they find in the caricatures she makes of their faces; the more marriage-friendly hours.

At home Tom is sprawled on the sofa, absorbed, papers littering the floor around him. She trails her hand across the back of his neck and he allows himself to be distracted, but only briefly.

"I need to get this report in by tomorrow."

The obvious regret in his voice affirms her. "Coffee?" She offers.

"Please, thanks." He stretches up to touch her shoulder, "I'll try not to be too long."

At the mirror in the hallway she pauses, puzzled. Her features are hazy, as if in soft focus. She opens her eyes wide and blinks twice, but the blurring remains. Beneath her breastbone, a flutter of fear replaces joy. She massages her stomach, thinks - Was I wrong to take the risk? In the morning after checking her blood sugar levels she stops in front of the mirror again and smiles experimentally: for the first time relieved to see fine lines appearing around her eyes, faint, but distinct. Her smile widens, genuine this time - it'll be ok.

The first performance of the day is a matinee. She flies through her list, retrieving the stored images from her memory and replicating them on each eager, up-turned face with familiar, expert strokes and from the rear of the theatre, as the scenes unfold under the spotlight glare, she feels a rush of satisfaction, seeing her bold, disproportionate lines transformed into age and character. But later, in the softer light of their hallway, her reflection is once again hazy, pitted with dark spots. - Perhaps the mirror has a flaw. The worm of fear uncurls in her stomach - I should check.

*   *   *

There are already four people in the eye department waiting area. Professional interest quickened, Sunetra scrutinises the faces of her co-victims, automatically logging tone, expression, the play of light and shade. Covertly she consults her watch, thinking of the line of kids waiting to be made-up, considers cancelling - perhaps it would be easier not to know.

And then it is her turn. As she reads the lines of letters on the wall chart she is puzzled afresh that she can make out the bottom line with ease, yet struggles to see the central letters on every line, even the biggest. She finds it extraordinarily difficult to sit in silence as the technician asks her to tilt her head this way and that, repeatedly flashing a light into each eye in turn. He waves her to another seat where she leans forwards, resting her chin on the curved support, her forehead pressed against a bar, while he photographs each eye in turn. He sits back, pushes the machine away from her, swings round to his desk, scribbles something in the folder that bears her name and glancing down at her stomach asks, "You're pregnant, is that right?"

She nods.

"How far on?"

"Eleven weeks."

"Hmm." He is touching his curled fist against his chin in rapid, short movements as if an aid to thought. A series of quick fire questions follow: about her general health, her diabetic control since she realised she was pregnant, her water works. And finally, her vision. "Any problems with dark spots?" She thinks of the mirror in the hallway, bites her lip. He gestures towards the wallchart and asks her to read the letters again, his eyes narrowing as she hesitates on the centre of each line.

His tone is neutral. "I need to run these tests again with your pupils dilated... As you probably know, pregnancy is an additional risk factor." She senses that he is choosing his next words with care, "And ethnicity." A pause, an additional gentleness, "Perhaps your husband could accompany you?"

Back in the waiting room, she makes a new appointment - I have to tell Tom.

*   *   *

When she first talked of trying for a baby Tom had raised the issue of risk, insisting *she* was more important. Sunetra had been combative: it wouldn't happen to them. She was good with her diabetic control. And when Tom remained unconvinced, when she stopped the pill without saying, she had told herself it would work out and he'd be pleased in the end. Now that it seems her gamble may have been lost she finds it impossible to confess, about the baby or the possible consequences, and so attends the appointment alone - when I know for sure, she thinks.

Her folder lies open on the table, the photographs graded. Today she has been assigned to the senior practicioner who is sympathetic, clear and blunt.

"Oh no, no…" she shakes her head, rejecting his diagnosis despite the words arrowing into her brain: haemorrhages… macular oedema… thickening of the retina… rapid progression. Treatment is urgent, the prognosis poor: six months at worst, perhaps two years. Reference is made again to her husband.

On the way home she buys elderflower cordial as a prelude to explaining to Tom, but can't find the words, her awkward, inconsequential chatter over their meal placing a new distance between them. So that afterwards he surrounds himself with papers, as if in protection. Maybe tomorrow, she thinks, touching her stomach, wondering how it might feel to hold her child, hold Tom, without seeing.

*　　*　　*

The artistic director pauses beside her as she works on the new cast list. "Why the hurry? Relax." He nods towards the names stuck around the edge of the mirror. "You've plenty of time."

But her new found speed is a symptom of a different fear: that her sight will fail, not with the slow fading of a dimmer switch, but without warning, like a blown light bulb. Her quota accomplished, she revisits them, picking characters at random, parading them in her mind, their markings bold and sharp. And at home sets herself a test: choosing a colour at random and shutting her eyes, ripples her fingers along the trays of her greasepaint box until she thinks she has found it. At first erratic, with practice she discovers she can guide her fingers by the colour wheel rotating in her head and choose aright. She searches through the debris of years for the life-size, rubber head - if I can manage, I can tell Tom. It's a long time since she used the head to practise, and never like this. When she opens her eyes to look at her first attempt: the features accidentally grotesque, the strokes of colour thick, without definition, silent tears slide down her cheeks - what if I can't, she thinks.

*   *   *

After three days of rain they wake to clear skies.

Tom says "Let's go to the beach. This might be our summer."

Stretched out above the high water mark Sunetra shuts her eyes, paints the picture into her memory: the out-going tide rolling up the shingle, lazily moving strands of seaweed, drifting them forwards, sucking them back, dropping them, purple-black on the damp sand. Surrounding the bay the rocks are lichen-covered, topped with moss and marram grass and spikes of bog cotton. The sun is hot on her eyelids, the sensation a comfort - I will always know when it is shining, she thinks. Tom is tracing a circle on the back of her hand, and as she opens her eyes he leans towards her, his experimental kiss feather-light - soon, she thinks. When I can prove I can cope.

*   *   *

She talks to the director, steeling herself against his shock, the disbelief and pity in his eyes.

'Of course you can try, but…'

She asks John, the closest of her co-workers to be her guinea-pig, sliding her fingers over his face, attempting to transmit to her brain by touch alone his line of jaw, the sweep of his cheekbones, the hollows around his eyes. It is an awkward extension of their friendship, in which she senses his equal unease. Yet when she finishes he offers,

"Again?"

"No." She slams the box shut, walks away. He catches up with her, touches her arm, draws her back. Her second attempt is better, and the third, the outcome an improvement, though not good enough… yet. On the way home she pauses at a play park to watch a tow-headed child jump from the climbing frame into his mother's arms - maybe not good enough ever, she thinks.

*   *   *

There are various possible treatments: laser, intravitreal steroids, growth factor drugs. She grins at that, briefly. All have downsides, none have guarantees. A pain re-inforced when at a bus stop a child in a pushchair drops her toy and Sunetra, retrieving it is rewarded by a smile - perhaps you can sense a smile, she thinks, her throat constricting. She phones the clinic. "I will try anything, everything you can offer."

It takes barely a week to make a creditable job on John's face. Encouraged, she tackles the house, re-organising it into clear spaces and straight lines, the replacement of their old, haphazard, comfortable kind of living an additional loss - perhaps Tom will guess, she thinks, stifling her guilt.

*   *   *

Treatment looming, she walks home by the river, the journey transmuted into a series of still photographs, pin-point sharp. A permanent collection to hang in the gallery of her mind: willows stirred by the wind, catkins dancing; a mallard floating on dappled water, ducklings strung out like beads behind her; a father and son on a bridge, playing at Pooh Sticks. It is a revelation - it's Tom's child too - today, she decides.

When she reaches the house he is already there, standing in the hallway, briefcase abandoned, staring at the re-arranged furniture, the new neatness of everything, a puzzled look on his face. She goes to him, curving under his arm, and capturing his other hand, brings it to rest on her stomach. "We need to talk," she says.

Sow the Wind…

The clinic, expensive even by the standards of fertility treatment, has a reputation for integrity, for success. When the consultant, his face a professional mask of sensitivity, leaves us alone for a few moments Caro stands up, her bag pressed against her chest, the signature leather dog dangling, blood red.

"Where are you going?" I say *(wrong words, wrong tone)*.

She stiffens.

I try again *(gently, gently)* "Please, Caro…"

She hesitates, but doesn't turn, her voice splintering, like the first fringe of ice on the edge of deep water. "I don't know."

I start to get up, but am pressed down again by her involuntary recoil. *(I want to hold you.)* Instead I try, "How long…?"

"I don't know," she repeats, still without turning.

On the table lies our crushed appointment slip and Caroline's gloves knotted into a ball, and the faint, retreating scent of 'Anais Anais' is carried to me in the draught from the closing door.

*   *   *

I remember that first day: Caroline - bright among the monochrome scaffy-jeans-clad matriculation queue that straggled around the hall. A pale blue and cream skirt flared above her knee, the soft-looking mottled jumper and flat shoes unfamiliar, strange. Later I came to recognize lovat and cashmere and bias-cut. Then I thought - *what a cracker, pity about the gear.* Yet found myself edging along the queue, guesstimating the quicker slots, narrowing the gap between us. Finally close, I logged her features: the lop-sided upturn of her mouth, a stray lock of hair falling over her ear, the misaligned eye-tooth. Each less than perfect; the whole, somehow, prettier. Irritated I spun from the queue, out of the door, down the steps. Half way across the road anger replaced irritation. I don't do retreat. I blagged and short-cutted my way back. Hovered. For her pen to run out, her papers to drop. Instead a clumsy shifting of my backpack sent her bag spinning to the floor. As I bent to retrieve it I was rewarded by a flash of thigh and a whiff of summer, but she was too quick and as she straightened, her gaze passed straight through me. Anger hardened into resolve.

*   *   *

We were on the same course, assigned to the same tutorial group, but I didn't know the codes, the norms of her universe. Didn't possess wellies, green or otherwise, for all that the wasteland on which I'd squandered my teens had been cratered and scarred with oil-slicked puddles like lakes. Where I came from wellies were for kids. And as for a chat-up line, I struggled to go beneath her accent, and she mine. But in the end I found a route - my understanding of 'Complex Analysis' and 'Linear Mathematics' clearer than hers and therefore useful. Payback was subtle. Chameleon-like I made small changes - striped lilac shirt, Pringle jumper, leather-laced loafers. Gradual alterations in the tone and content of my speech, which became, in aggregate, significant. Shedding the 'Before-Caroline' life like an outgrown skin, my transformation was finally confirmed in the pre-finals 'milk-round', when I landed a coveted accountancy place with Deloitte and Touche.

"Fate" she said, flicking at my newly grown fringe.

Love was easy, cocooned, as we were, in our out of the way corner of Scottish academia, where no planes landed, and even the train line was a miles-away, wind-swept halt. Where 'Afterwards' was long ignored, until, finally, emerging into our new, fast-forward lifestyle, we allowed our families to collide in a flurry of flowers and champagne; the distinction between 'Moss Bros' and 'Magee' blurred, in retrospect, by photographic skill. They separated with a forced politeness on each side, allied to an equal thankfulness for the geographic distance between them.

She was the third in a family of four, the last to marry. Early on I said, thinking of the already five grandchildren, the christening just attended, "At least there's no pressure on us."

And knew immediately it was the wrong thing to say.

For eighteen months we were happy - an inadequate description, but the alternatives: ecstatic, delirious, seem greedy. Then Caroline started counting, calculating, phoning, so that I rushed home at odd hours, to copulate briefly and without romance. The memory surfaced, refused to be quashed: the tired cubicle, a Philippino nurse whisking away my bottle; the welcome cash.

We took holidays in hot, out-of-the-way, exclusive places: days crammed with leisure, nights with desperate love. And home again, parried the covert glances, the un-asked questions, began to avoid our more 'blessed' friends.

A new phase: strategically-placed magazines left open at relevant articles, and engineered invitations to dinner from little-known couples who'd had 'difficulties', happily now passed. The meal over, the wife would whisk Caroline away to admire the sleeping child, while the husband, awkward, talked of cricket and the stock exchange and, hurriedly, as we heard them returning, of how it was 'so worth it', how it had 'changed their life'.

My leaflet drop: internet-sourced copies of 'Be My Parent', produced only distance between us, so I tried another, more honest, tactic.

"Perhaps it would be better not to know." *(I want to spare you this.)*

"It's the not knowing that's the hell."

Defeated, I said, "If you're sure, really sure."

"Yes" she said, touching my face, pulling my mouth into a smile.

We chose a clinic.

"Everyone does it," she said, misinterpreting *(how could she do otherwise)* my reluctance to go for tests. She pulled me against her, moulding her pelvis into mine, eyes darkening to violet. "This is Nothing to do with being a Man."

*   *   *

We haven't slept. At six am she curls into me, tracing a circle on my stomach.

"Suppose he says…" she begins, and I feel her fear like a weight.

"Shush." I say, trusting my hands to whisper the comfort I cannot voice. I know what the consultant will say, and have been practising reassurance, in all its guises, for weeks now.

Her eyes are luminous, the pupils edged with irises stretched into fine blue lines, her bottom lip caught between her teeth. "Are you afraid?"

"Yes" I say. *(For you, my love.)*

With the tip of her finger she draws a line from my throat to my navel. "So am I."

In return I move my hand in an exploratory, questioning gesture; feel her respond to my touch. Afterwards, lying slack and heavy, my jaw resting on her shoulder, I make one last attempt,

"We don't need to go…"

She jerks away, the air between us fragile with longing. "They'll be able to do *something*."

"Yes," I say again. *(What else can I say?)*

*   *   *

It is our third visit to the clinic, the one in which we will get our results. Dressing with customary care, she lays out clothes for me also: a throwback to the early days, and I put them on without protest. (*I owe her that.*)

We pass through the gated archway, scrunch to a halt on the sweep of gravel . At the top of the steps she pauses, her voice far away. "I want this."

"I know."

"If it's me?"

"I'll love you whatever," I say, too quickly.

"You can't know that."

I hear the ragged edge in her voice, feel a matching almost-despair. (*But oh my love, I do know*) "I promise," I say.

"I do too."

We cross the hallway - an expensive blend of polished oak and marble crowned by a stucco frieze with an over-abundance of fruits spilling a riot of fecundity and colour. I risk a glance at Caro: she's staring at me, as if she seeks to memorize my face, the hunger in her eyes arrow-sharp.

*   *   *

I hold her hand as the consultant talks statistics - sperm count, blood tests, scans; his pen an accusing finger indicating where and how we

139

deviate from the normative range. And for perhaps the first time I hate the clarity of mathematics. I focus on nodding at appropriate points, aware of Caroline's stricken face beside me, try *(let me at least get this right)* to anticipate just enough to tighten my grip when she needs it most.

"I'll leave you to consider," he says, fixing his gaze on a point somewhere above and beyond Caroline's right ear. "A high sperm count is very positive." Then with a glance at me, "Take your time."

I turn to Caro, try to draw her close, to touch away the hurt. This I have been practising from the start. "We have a chance.*"*

She raises her eyes to mine and I see her pain shifting, from guilt, through bewilderment, to sudden, terrible comprehension.

"You knew." She pulls back, sucking in accusation and incredulity in equal measure, "You knew."

"I'm sorry." *(What else can I say?)*

"How" she says, abrading the space between us.

"It was a long time ago…"

She shakes her head, looks away.

"Not a person." *(Easy money, a bit of a laugh. A macho thing, in retrospect, tawdry.)*

Her gaze swings sharply back.

"I can hardly remember." *(But I do remember - all too clearly - the acres of plate glass, sunlight bouncing off the metal frames, the inside coolness a physical blow. The tiled cubicle, the piles of well-thumbed magazines that I thought at first, in my pride, I wouldn't need.)*

One hand is at her throat. "When?"

"Before you." *(A lifetime before you.)*

"When?" she repeats, radiating insistence.

"Between school and Uni." *(After the fruit factory, travelling with mates, spending more, much more than we could afford. The poster in the campus bar . "Bet you a fiver I'll be first." "Tenner, you won't.")*

"Where?"

"Does that matter?"

A how-can-you-even-ask look, a hard edge in her voice. "Where?"

I think of lying, the truth quicksand. "Boston." *(Afterwards, snacking, American-style, in Faneuil Hall, clam chowder in a bread bowl, the mothers and babies that surrounded us providing a temporary reality.)*

"We've been there." A pause, drawn-out. "We might have seen…"

"Caro… please…" *(Don't think of that.)* Her arms are crossed against her chest, as if for protection. I try to re-capture her hands, but she resists, curling them into fists and I wish she

141

would hit me, scream at me, anything, other than this white-faced rigidity.

"We gave blood too," I offer.

A small, should-that-make-it-better sound, then, "How many?"

"I don't know." *(I've never wondered until now.)*

She weighs it up, a nerve pulsing beneath her eye.

"But you knew this. All these years. All these weeks. All your 'ifs' and 'I'll love you whatevers'. All the time you knew. You knew it was me."

When I don't reply *(what can I say?)* she stands up, pushs back the smart upholstered chair, "You should have told me…"

Outside in the corridor I hear people passing backwards and forwards, brisk footsteps clicking on the marble floor. "I love you," I say. *(If you only knew how much I love you.)*

"Oh, love…" she repeats, stretching it into a sigh. Her eyes drop to the papers on the desk, a distant ache in her voice, "You think love is enough?" Bending, she scoops up the sheaf of graphs and charts and shreds them into confetti, scattering it on the carpet around our feet.

"Please…"

The final hesitation, her eyes fixed on the door, as if she too concentrated on the external commonplace - the disembodied voices and fractured conversations, the rustle of starched cotton against nylon, the background hum of a floor-polisher. But she doesn't turn, only feels for the door handle as if blind, and is gone.

*   *   *

I have a crumpled appointment slip and Caroline's gloves knotted into a ball and the faint, retreating scent of 'Anais Anais' captured in the draught from the closing door.

But I don't know what I'll have when I get home.

Working Away

The agency man is talking, insistent as a mosquito. "This is how it will be. Where you will go. Very nice people. Very good room. It will be very fine."

Mmberane pauses, curious only. He notes the dark suit, the crisp, white shirt, and reaches for his own, newly bought handkerchief, shaking it out and raising it to his brow. The feel of the stiff cotton sings to him: *Today I have begun.*

On the brow of the hill he stops, breathing deeply, and again mops his forehead, the handkerchief already limp. Below him the village slumbers, the contours softened by the heat, the cluster of circular huts mud-brown daubs against the smear of earth and sky. In the corner of his eye he catches a streak of yellow followed by red, a shout, a tumble, high-pitched laughter carried to him in the still air. He lifts his bag, empty now but for the roll of sacking and his money purse, and slings it over his shoulder, his chest swelling at the clink of coins.

Iminza has seen him and comes running, her dress lifting and spinning as she leaps up and wraps her legs and arms around him. Saliku tugs at his trouser leg, poking a stubby finger through the hole at the back of the knee.

"Aaie!" Mmberane shifts Iminza onto one hip, bends and swings Saliku up onto the other, presses them close, tells them, "Daddy has sold everything today." He bounces them up and down as he strides along the track, so that they squeal and cling tight. It is mid-afternoon, the village quiet, almost deserted. Only the old remain, resting in the shade of their huts, and those of the children either too young or too poor to go to school. He knows the talk: that he will never amount to anything, that Grace made a mistake in marrying him, and feels a stab of regret: he should have lingered, come home late when all would see the empty sack, his bulging purse.

He is kneeling by the bed, dragging out the carved box that lies beneath, as Grace enters. She pauses in the doorway, hesitant. Sensing in her stillness the apprehension that she is too loyal to express, he turns towards her, rocking on his heels and beaming reassurance. He holds out the purse.

"I thought…" She weighs it in her hand, her dark eyes damp, and he reaches for her, buries her face in his chest, leans his chin on the tight fuzz of her hair.

"Ninety shillings," he says, tightening his grip. "This year" he says, "this year we will be very fine." His finger traces the line of her spine, his hand coming to rest in the small of her back. "I feel it."

The next day is good also, and the next, and each night as Grace curves into him, welcoming, he responds without reserve. It is three o'clock on Friday when he makes his last sale: to a woman in a mission handout, the pattern faded under the armpits, one of the buttons on the front mismatched. He has six good potatoes left, round and firm, weighing heavy. He is already adding the final ten shillings to the total in his head as she hesitates, puts her hand in her pocket as if counting the coins there, then holds out her string bag,

"Four," she says, her chin tilting.

He drops them in, asks for seven shillings. As he waits, he sees Grace in a similar dress, though her hem never drags. "Here," he thrusts the remaining two potatoes into the bag, avoids her eyes, fans his face, "Aaie… it is too hot and who would want only two?"

He brushes away her mumbled 'Asante', embarrassed by her thanks, and stretches, rolling up the sacking, tucking it under his arm as he drifts around the market stalls. Many things tempt him, yet each time he pauses, he jingles the money in his purse, looks, shakes his head in dismissal; passes on. It is a fine thing to be able to choose not to buy. He lingers longest under a sign proclaiming 'The best batik-maker in Serem'. The stall-holder unfurls the fabric with a practised tug, the colours blending and swirling before him. Stroking the bright cottons he imagines Grace: the pattern cascading from her shoulder, over her breasts, cradling her smooth, slightly rounded stomach, the curve of her thighs. He reaches for his purse, hesitates, blurts out,

"Next month… my wife… it is her birthday - I will come then."

The agency man is there again, in the corner where the stalls peter out into an open area cluttered with ancient bicycles, rickety ox-carts and the occasional dust-covered, dented van. This time he rests one foot on the runner of a gleaming matatu; his vowels stretched, sinuous.

"Very good hotel. Very good tips. It will be very fine."

A man steps forward and hands over a clutch of notes before swinging his bag onto the minibus roof rack and joining those already seated inside. Watching, Mmberane thinks of how the man will come home only two or three times a year, that his wife, his children will be strangers to him, and is thankful that he has no schooling, no certificate.

Grace is cross-legged on the floor, a dress for Iminza spread on her lap, a handful of pins sticking from her mouth. She is pressing the fabric with her fingers, smoothing out the gathers around the waist, pinning, tucking. It is a pretty dress of turquoise satin, embroidered flowers scattered across the skirt, but Mmberane brushes it aside, gently removes the pins from her lips, cradles her hands, elation in his voice.

"This week, two hundred and eighty shillings. Next month," he squeezes her fingers, "the beans will be ready and who knows…" He picks up the dress, closes his hand over the label at the neck, hiding the English name in faded ink. "Soon," he says, "Soon I will buy new." Grace leans into him and he feels her heartbeat, and lower down another flutter. He steps back, searches her face, sees the hope shining.

"I wasn't sure. Not till today. But I think we will be blessed again." For a moment a shadow crosses her face. "If all is well."

He rests his hand on her stomach, "It will be. It will be very well."

He carries the beans to market, a swing in his step. His usual pitch is taken, but he finds a space, stretching out his sacking, setting up the scales, lining up the stones as weights. On one side of him an old woman, as scrawny as the three chickens that squawk and peck in a crate at her feet, and on the other, a man with his head bent over a whetstone, feeling for the edge, the knife in his hand sliding and lifting, sliding and lifting in continuous motion.

From the woman Mmberane's 'Jambo' elicits a toothless smile, deepening the creases in her face, while the knife-sharpener tilts his head towards the voice, his eyes opaque as an overcast sky. Mmberane shifts on his haunches, makes a surreptitious sign of the cross, but stays his ground. Afterwards, walking home as the heat bleeds out of the sun, he dismisses the superstition and instead blames the good harvest, the many other bean-sellers, that a third of his crop lies limp in his bag, that his purse is light.

The next day he leaves before dawn to claim a different pitch, prays his luck will change. But though it is not a bad week, it is not a good one either, and each evening he hurries past the batik stall, head down, reminding himself that there are still two weeks until Grace's birthday. And at the foot of the market he skirts the perimeter to avoid the stall with the accusing line of girl's dresses strung out like gaily-coloured flags.

But he cannot avoid the agency man, persuading his clients into the comfort of the matatu, his voice repetitive as a recording. "...Where you will go... What you will do. Very good people... It will be very fine." Unable to resist Mmberane stops, watches the flash of gold in his mouth, listens. Sees the pictures: summer-bright, many-coloured, like finest batik.

He has almost decided, but has given himself one last day. It is cooler now and though there are people enough, few stop, those who do buying little, haggling hard. He must carry many things away again and when they have paid for the school for Mbone there will be less in the box, not more.

Afterwards, when he has signed the papers, he walks home, each turn in the path a private goodbye. Outside their hut Grace is preparing their evening meal: steamed cassava, sweet potatoes, kidney beans. Soon, he thinks, soon she will be able to have chicken also. Inside he drags out the box, unlocking it with the key tied on a string under his shirt. Carefully he counts: the agency man requires 1200 shillings for travel, 600 for uniform, 250 commission. He thinks of the very fine room, the very good job, a salary.

All around him are the sounds of evening: wives cooking, children playing, insects buzzing. He hears the rhythmic slap, stamp, slap as Iminza skips, the frayed rope-ends twisted around her palms. Mbone throws small stones towards a series of circles scratched in the dust and Saliku, squatting beside them, squeals each time one reaches the target. Mmberane thinks of marbles, of a sturdy, rainbow-coloured rope. And for a moment only, of stifling heat, canned music, hooting horns. There is a pain beneath his breastbone, but he thrusts it away.

The agency man has said the matatu will leave at eight. Mmberane knows it will not; still he will not risk being late. He thinks of the hotel in Mombasa where he will open doors and carry cases, of the fat tips from wealthy tourists, of his first wage. He thinks of a dress for Iminza, the cloth for Grace. He thinks of later, when he has saved enough to bring his family to a fine house: where Grace will cook indoors, where their mattress will not be stuffed with rags. He thinks of school for all his children and of the beach where he will watch them play, curling their toes around the warm sand.

He refuses to think of the stories he has heard.

If you have enjoyed these stories, please consider leaving a review or contact the author to provide feedback via her website at www.margaretskea.com

Also by Margaret Skea

The Munro series:

Historical novels set in 16th century Scotland.

Scotland 1586. An ancient feud threatens Munro's home, his family, even his life.

Munro owes allegiance to the Cunninghames and to the Earl of Glencairn. He escapes the bloody aftermath of a massacre, but cannot escape the disdain of the wife he sought to protect, nor inner conflict, as he wrestles with his conscience, with divided loyalties and, most dangerous of all, a growing friendship with the rival Montgomerie clan.

Set against the backdrop of the turmoil of the closing years of the sixteenth century, *Turn of the Tide* follows the fortunes of a fictional family trapped at the centre of a notorious historic feud, known as the Ayrshire Vendetta. Beginning in the 15th century and not finally resolved until the latter part of the 17th, the Cunninghames and Montgomeries were dubbed the 'Montagues and Capulets' of Ayrshire.

153

Praise for Turn of the Tide

'I thought the quality of the writing and the research were outstanding.'

Jeffrey Archer

'Margaret Skea brings the 16th century to vivid life.'

Sharon K Penman

'Munro frames the book, in at the initial kill, and centre stage in the brilliant climax, all the more shocking as the conclusion of an otherwise measured tale... a fascinating and engaging read with great visual effect.'

Bristol Writers

'It is hard to know where to begin, there were so many things I liked about *Turn of the Tide*... an emotionally gripping story about a man caught between duty and conscience at a time in history when a man's livelihood depended upon his loyalty to family and clan.'

The History Lady

'I have read some wonderful debut novels this year - *Turn of the Tide* is one of them. I loved it... a tale of love, loyalty, tragedy and betrayal.'

Books Please

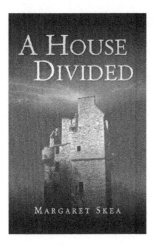

Ayrshire 1597. The truce between the Cunninghame and Montgomerie clans is fragile. And for the Munro family, living in hiding under assumed names, these are dangerous times.

While Munro risks his life daily in the army of the French King, the spectre of discovery by William Cunninghame haunts his wife Kate. Her fears for their children and her absent husband realized as William's desire for revenge tears their world apart.

A sweeping tale of compassion and cruelty, treachery and sacrifice, set against the backdrop of a religious war, feuding clans and the Great Scottish Witch Hunt of 1597.

This eagerly awaited sequel to *Turn of the Tide* can also be read as a stand-alone novel and will appeal to fans of Winston Graham's Poldark and C J Sansom's Shardlake series.

Praise for A House Divided

'Captivating and fast-paced. You'll find yourself reading far into the night.

Ann Weisgarber

(Walter Scott and Orange Prize shortlisted author of *The Promise*)

'A classic adventure that grips from the very first page.'

Shirley McKay

(Author of the Hew Cullen mystery series.)

'Expertly narrated… full of tension and surprises. It's strong, compelling reading, one of the best books I've read this year.'

Books Please

'Compelling plot, well-developed characters… a gripping, fantastic read.'

Helen Hollick – Vine Voice

(Due for publication Summer 2018)

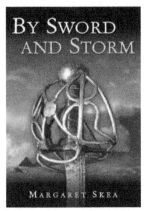

France 1598. As the French Wars of Religion draw to a close the Edict of Nantes establishes religious freedom in all but Paris. For Kate Munro in Picardie the child she carries symbolizes a new life free from past troubles, while in Scotland Elizabeth Montgomerie yearns both for a son and heir and for peace. When Adam Munro foils an attempt on the French king's life and the family is called to court, Kate prays that their children will benefit. But Paris holds dangers as well as delights and for both families there are troubled times ahead.

Praise for By Sword and Storm

'Two interconnected storylines are threaded into this fast paced novel, with colourful individuals, opulent settings and clashes of personality aplenty. A hugely satisfying read.'

Undiscovered Scotland

The Katharina series
Novels based on the life of Katharina von Bora

Germany 1505. Five-year-old Katharina is placed in the convent at Brehna. She will never see her father again.

Sixty-five miles away, at Erfurt, Martin Luder, a promising young law student, turns his back on a lucrative career to become a monk.

The consequences of their meeting in Wittenberg, on Easter Sunday 1523, will reverberate down the centuries and throughout the Christian world.

A compelling portrayal of Katharina von Bora, set against the turmoil of the Peasant's War and the German Reformation … and the controversial priest at its heart.

Praise for Katharina: Deliverance

'Margaret Skea has a brilliant eye for historical detail. She creates characters who take us by the hand so that we never stumble or wonder where we are. An engrossing read.'

Between the Lines

'A wonderfully vivid portrait. Skea knows her history, but more importantly, she writes with imagination and humanity.'

Prof. Alec Ryrie, Durham University (Author of *Protestants*)

(Due for publication early 2019)

Continues the story of Katharina as she handles the pressures of death threats, miscarriage, the loss of of two of her children, several outbreaks of plague, and the devastating effects of war. She organises the printing of much of Luther's writings, copes with his many illnesses and bouts of depression and moderates his overly-generous impulses, to the detriment of her own reputation.

Following Luther's unexpected death she has to fight to retain her inheritance and her independence; and provide for and protect her children from the continuing conflicts and outbreaks of plague, one of which ultimately led to her own death.